Nikki's skin looked pale and translucent in the moonlight, her eyes dark and unfathomable.

Something stirred inside Adam. Something unexpected and completely unwise. Maybe even dangerous, considering the circumstances.

"You looked a lot different back then," he said.

"Which is why my friends and I were scapegoated." She scowled into the night. "If you were around that summer, you must have heard those rumors, too."

"About wild rumors? Yeah."

She gave him a sidelong glance. "You aren't afraid to be alone with me out here?"

"Not for a second."

His conviction seemed to rattle her. "Maybe you should be."

He pointed to the scar at his scalp. "Foolish or not, I'm not that easily spooked."

A DESPERATE SEARCH

AMANDA STEVENS

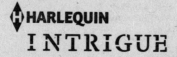

HARLEQUIN
INTRIGUE

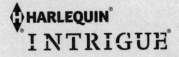

Recycling programs
for this product may
not exist in your area.

ISBN-13: 978-1-335-13661-9

A Desperate Search

This is a work of fiction. Names, characters, places and incidents
are either the product of the author's imagination or are used fictitiously.
Any resemblance to actual persons, living or dead, businesses,
companies, events or locales is entirely coincidental.

This edition published by arrangement with Harlequin Books S.A.

For questions and comments about the quality of this book,
please contact us at CustomerService@Harlequin.com.

Harlequin Enterprises ULC
22 Adelaide St. West, 40th Floor
Toronto, Ontario M5H 4E3, Canada
www.Harlequin.com

Printed in U.S.A.

Amanda Stevens is an award-winning author of over fifty novels, including the modern gothic series The Graveyard Queen. Her books have been described as eerie and atmospheric, and "a new take on the classic ghost story." Born and raised in the rural South, she now resides in Houston, Texas, where she enjoys binge-watching, bike riding and the occasional margarita.

Books by Amanda Stevens

Harlequin Intrigue

An Echo Lake Novel

Without a Trace
A Desperate Search

Twilight's Children

Criminal Behavior
Incriminating Evidence
Killer Investigation

Pine Lake
Whispering Springs

Bishop's Rock (ebook novella)

MIRA Books

The Graveyard Queen

The Restorer
The Kingdom
The Prophet
The Visitor
The Sinner
The Awakening

Visit the Author Profile page at Harlequin.com.

CAST OF CHARACTERS

Nikki Dresden—When her mentor turns up dead, the Nance County coroner worries that something dark has been going on in Belle Pointe, Texas, right under her nose.

Adam Thayer—A strange phone call leads a big-city detective to a small-town killer...and to an enigmatic woman from his past.

Lila Wilkes—A lonely widow with a secret past has ingratiated herself so thoroughly in Belle Pointe that she is now considered the town's guardian angel.

Dr. Patience Wingate—The deceased's ex-lover and business partner seems desperate to cover her tracks.

Dessie Dupre—She was the deceased's faithful housekeeper for over thirty years...until a smooth attorney with a secret agenda sweeps her off her feet.

Clete Darnell—The deceased's attorney charms an older woman destined to inherit a fortune.

Eddie Bowman—This junkman has dabbled in drugs, blackmail and now possibly murder for hire.

Chapter One

The sun dipped beneath the dense pine forest, casting long shadows across Echo Lake. Thankfully, the temperature had dropped from the midday high of triple digits, but the air was still hot and muggy, with barely a breeze stirring the long tresses of Spanish moss that shrouded the bank. Beyond the shade, in a patch of lingering sunlight, water lilies unfurled in the heat. From this thick carpet of aquatic vegetation, cypress stumps rose like an army of gnomes to form a circle around the rotting corpse.

Nikki Dresden was glad she'd hauled down her waders from the road along with her kit. The body floated facedown just beyond reach of the bank. She tried not to think about the moccasins and gators that nested in the cattails as she sloshed through the shallow water. The smell of decay wafted on the breeze, making her also glad for the spare clothing and sneakers she kept in a duffel in her SUV. She wasn't shy about stripping. The navy coveralls she wore now would go in a garbage bag that would be placed in an airtight container for transport back to either the laundry at the lab or the heavy-duty washing machine on her back porch. Nikki had learned early on in her career as the Nance County coroner that once the scent of death invaded the close confines of a vehicle, the odor would linger for days if not weeks. Now she took precautions in every aspect of her job.

Which was why, upon arrival at the lake, she'd spent the first few minutes scribbling notes and sketching the topography and layout of the scene before donning her gear. Nuances were critical and memory unreliable. Even photographs could later create a false perception. A capsized fishing boat underneath the bridge suggested an accidental drowning, but Nikki knew better than to make a snap, uninformed declaration. What appeared to be an accident might later prove otherwise, and investigators had one shot at processing the scene.

The first responders had secured the area and Sheriff Tom Brannon had kept law enforcement personnel to a minimum. The crime scene unit searched up and down the bank while a young officer named Billy Navarro took photographs and another officer shot video. The deputies who had arrived late to the scene watched from the top of the embankment. A man Nikki didn't know sat on a log just outside the perimeter. She assumed he was the one who had reported the body. She'd given him a curious glance as she pulled on the waders and had found him staring back at her. She couldn't place him, and yet his straightforward regard had unsettled her. Had they met before?

The question niggled at the back of her mind as she focused on the business at hand. At least it was still daylight, though dusk hovered at the edges of the pink horizon. Night creatures already stirred on the opposite bank, the distant serenade of bullfrogs and crickets mingling with the relentless buzz of the blowflies that had homed in on the corpse once it rose to the surface.

Off to the right, she caught the glide of something sinewy and silent in her periphery. The lake here was deeper than she'd thought. Stepping off a ledge, she felt cool liquid ooze into the waders, making it difficult to navigate the muddy bottom. She trudged on, trying not to think about what might have slithered in with the water.

Sheriff Brannon called to her from the bank. "Sure you don't need some help?"

"I'm good." She tried to keep her balance as she flicked a mosquito from her eyelash. The last thing she wanted was to fall on her butt in front of a bunch of snickering deputies, but the lake bed was slippery, the waders cumbersome, and Nikki had never been known for her grace. She grabbed one of the cypress stumps and propelled herself forward.

"What do you see?" the sheriff asked.

The body bobbled as she pushed closer. "Victim is male Caucasian. Gray hair, slender build. Older man, the best I can tell."

"Any idea how long he's been in the water? Or who he is?"

"All I can say for certain is that the body is bloated and floating." Meaning as the corpse had decomposed underwater, the release of gases had caused him to rise to the surface.

"Gotcha," Tom said. "What about wounds?"

"Nothing visible. The arms and legs are still partially submerged. I can't see much more than the back of his head and torso." Nikki took a camera from a waterproof bag and snapped a few shots before she glanced back at the sheriff. "Let's get him to the bank."

The stranger rose as if intent on offering assistance. Instead, he paced back and forth for a moment before resuming his place on the log. He seemed…not exactly nervous, but on edge for some reason. Finding a dead body could do that to a person. His gaze remained fixed on the water. Was he looking at her or the corpse? Nikki wondered.

Don't flatter yourself.

Decked out as she was in rubber waders and shapeless coveralls, hair pulled back in a sloppy bun, face red and sweaty from the heat and humidity, she was more a curiosity than an attraction. Female coroners were still something of a rarity in rural East Texas.

"I'll need the hook," she called.

Billy Navarro set aside his camera and extended a telescopic pole out over the water. Nikki grabbed the end and affixed one of the prongs to the victim's belt. As two of the officers pulled, she tried to guide the body through the tangle of hydrilla and lily pads in order to minimize further damage and to preserve what might be left of any trace evidence.

Once they had him on the bank, the smell intensified in the steamy heat. One of the deputies coughed and turned his head. Another gagged. Nikki hunkered beside the body, relieved to be back on dry land as she took note of decomposition, animal predation and pruning in the deceased's hands.

"No identification?" Tom crouched on the other side of the body and waved aside a fly.

"Not in the back pockets," Nikki said. "Wallet may have fallen out in the water. Let's turn him over."

Tom motioned for help and the two officers who had manned the hook moved in to assist in rolling the victim and then backed out of the way. The water had done a number on the victim's face. His blanched features were so distorted he could have been a complete stranger lying on the bank beneath a feathery canopy of cypress leaves. He wasn't a stranger, though. The twinkle in the blue eyes had frosted, but the nose, the mouth, the small caduceus tattoo on the inner left wrist sent an icy shiver down Nikki's spine. Recognition knocked her back on her heels.

Billy Navarro leaned over Tom's shoulder. He was young and inexperienced, but he handled himself with far more poise than some of the seasoned deputies at the top of the embankment who were still struggling to keep down their last meals. "*Madre de Dios.* Is that who I think he is?"

Tom nodded. "Kind of hard to tell with all the bloating. Something's been gnawing on him, too. But I'd swear on my daddy's grave that's Charles Nance."

"It's him." Nikki touched a gloved finger to the dead man's wrist. "I recognize the tattoo. He once told me he got it on a dare during med school. His watch usually covered it."

Tom Brannon swore under his breath as Billy moved in for a closer look. "This is bad, Sheriff. Really bad. This man delivered me. My grandmother said I came early and my mother and I would have both died if not for Dr. Nance." He spoke with a note of reverence and fear, as if that fragile connection might somehow cause the dead man's misfortune to transfer to him.

"Yours isn't the only life he saved," Tom said. "His death will be a blow to the whole community." He glanced up then and caught Nikki's expression. His voice lowered. "Sorry, Nikki. I wish you hadn't had to see him like this. You two were pretty tight, weren't you?"

"He was like a grandfather to me," she said numbly. "A mentor, a hero. A drill sergeant when I needed one. I wouldn't have made it through med school without him."

Tom nodded. "I know how you feel. He helped out a lot of people in this county. He was a hero to many of us."

Nikki fell silent as she gulped in air. Already she could feel grief gnawing away at the shock of disbelief. Sheriff Brannon meant well, but there was no way he or anyone else could understand the depth of Nikki's loss. Charles Nance had not only been a friend and mentor, but one of the few people in the town of Belle Pointe, Texas, to ever give her the time of day. She'd grown up a misfit and loner, a troubled girl who'd flirted with darkness and courted disaster. When Tom's father had considered her a suspect in the disappearances of two of her classmates, Dr. Nance had stepped in and set the first Sheriff Brannon straight.

You're barking up the wrong tree, Porter. You and I both know you're targeting this girl and her friends solely for the way they choose to present themselves. Wearing black doesn't make them bad kids. Nor does the music they listen to. Nikki's been through a lot and

*is coping the best way she knows how. I suggest you
back off if you don't want to find yourself on the wrong
end of a malicious harassment suit.*

Nikki had been astounded by his passionate defense.
With the exception of her real grandfather, who had
died when she was nine, she'd never had anyone take
up for her the way Dr. Nance had. He'd cared enough
to look beyond the dyed hair and heavy makeup, beyond the sullen demeanor and the chip on her shoulder.
Maybe he'd seen a younger version of himself in Nikki.
He'd taken her under his wing, encouraged her interest in science and had been instrumental in helping to
secure the scholarships and grants that had made the
dream of college and medical school a reality. His influence on her life had been immeasurable. His death
would be the same. It would be days, months, perhaps
even years, before Nikki would be able to process the
impact.

She drew another breath as reality settled heavily
around her heart. "This doesn't make sense. He spent
a lot of time out here on the lake. He loved to boat and
fish. He was an excellent swimmer."

"Anything can happen on the water," Tom said. "Especially if you're out here alone. He was getting on up
there in years."

"Seventy-three," Nikki murmured. "With no sign
of slowing down."

"Maybe that was the problem. He could have had a
heart attack or stroke. Who knows?" Tom's shrug was
far from nonchalant. "But it does make you wonder
why no one called in a report. You and I both know he's

been in the water for days. Someone must have missed him. Friends, patients, his housekeeper. Someone."

"They probably thought he was out of town. He told me last week he was headed to Houston for a medical conference. He planned to take a few extra days to get in some deep-sea fishing out of Galveston while he was down that way. But none of that explains how he ended up here."

"Last-minute change of plans, maybe? It happens. How did he seem to you?"

Nikki thought about that final meeting and Dr. Nance's usual ribbing.

Sure you won't humor an old man and come with me? This time next week we can be out to sea, not a care between us. Might even go out deep enough to catch a big blue. Unlike my patients, yours won't complain if you take a little time off.

"He seemed in a fine mood." She tried to control the tremor in her voice. "He was looking forward to that fishing expedition in the Gulf."

"No hint of trouble? No health complaints? Nothing out of the ordinary that you can remember?"

Nikki paused. Had he seemed distracted or was that hindsight playing tricks? Had he looked a little pale, been a little subdued despite his usual teasing?

"Not that I noticed at the time," she said. "But I was in a hurry to get back to work and now I'm second-guessing that whole conversation. Maybe he was sick."

"Don't do that to yourself. There could be any number of explanations as to why he changed his plans. Maybe he backed out of the conference and decided to hide out at the lake for some R & R. God knows he deserved to." Tom trailed his gaze over the water. "I'll check with the conference registration about a cancellation. If his vehicle is at the cabin, that'll tell us something about his plans. Maybe we'll find his wallet and watch there, too. In any case, I think you should let Dr. Ramirez handle the autopsy."

She nodded her agreement. In addition to her duties as the Nance County coroner, Nikki also worked as one of three full-time pathologists at the Northeast Texas Forensic Science Center. In the state of Texas, any death that couldn't be explained by medical history or visual examination required an autopsy. The lab serviced all the rural counties in the Piney Woods area, so she and her colleagues stayed busy.

"I still can't believe he's gone." She was no stranger to loss. Her beloved grandfather was long dead and the grandmother who raised her had passed away two years ago. Her parents were still alive, as far as she knew, but she hadn't seen or heard from either in years. Now Dr. Nance was gone, too.

"It'll take some time to sink in," Tom said. "Memorial Hospital won't be the same without him. His great-granddaddy built the original hospital. There's been a Nance in charge for as long as anyone can remember. Hell, the Nances were some of the first settlers in these parts. His death coming so soon after all that other trouble…" He shook his head. "The community's already on edge and people tend to think the worst when something like this happens. We need to head off speculation before the rumor mill starts to grind. We owe Dr. Nance that much. I'd like to call a press conference as soon as possible. Be a good idea if you were there, too."

Nikki glanced across the body to where Tom still hunkered. She shuddered at the very notion of speaking to reporters about Dr. Nance's death. "Wouldn't it be better to wait until after the postmortem?"

"When will that be, do you think?"

"I'll talk to Dr. Ramirez about prioritizing the schedule, but tomorrow is Friday and we're swamped. It'll probably be Monday morning at the earliest."

"The news will be all over town by then," Tom said, worried. "I don't want to let people stew about it all weekend. At the very least, I'll need to issue a statement. I've got a little pull with the paper these days. They'll accommodate us as best they can in both the print and online editions."

Nikki nodded, vaguely aware of his impending nuptials to Rae Cavanaugh, whose relatives owned the *Echo Lake Star*. But her attention was caught once again by the stranger's brooding scrutiny. "What's his story?"

"He told one of my officers that he was walking along the lake when he spotted the body."

It was hard to read Tom's expression behind his mirrored sunglasses, but something in his voice troubled Nikki. "You don't believe him?"

"I've no reason not to."

"Then why that tone?"

Tom's mouth tightened. "We've had our share of trouble in Nance County. Drug trafficking, disappearances, murder. I guess I'm just naturally wary of strangers who happen upon dead bodies. But then, he's not really a stranger."

"He isn't?" Nikki tried to catch a glimpse of the man from the corner of her eye. She saw him rise from his perch on the log and rotate his arms as if to loosen kinked muscles. Then he moved up to the perimeter, leaning a shoulder against the nearest tree trunk as he slipped his hands in his pockets, all the while never taking his eyes off the corpse. Unlike some of the officers, he didn't seem affected by the smell or the condition of the deceased. On first glance, his body language appeared almost apathetic, but there was tension in his neck and shoulders and something darker than curiosity in the gleam of his eyes.

He was close enough now that Nikki felt the need to lower her voice to a near whisper. "Who is he? How do you know him?"

"I only know of him," Tom said. "His name is Adam Thayer. He just moved into his grandmother's old house on the other side of the bridge."

She stared at him in surprise. "He's Betsy Thayer's grandson?" Was that how she knew him? Had she caught a glimpse of him at one time or another when he'd come to see his grandmother? "I thought the family put her home on the market after she died."

"I doubt they got any bites," Tom said. "Prime location for a fishing retreat, but the place needs a lot of work. The fact that it was used to hide a kidnapping victim probably didn't add to the appeal. Come to think of it, maybe it's a good thing Thayer will be living there for a while. Empty houses tend to attract criminal activity."

"Not just houses."

"No, not just houses."

They turned as one, lifting their heads to the top of the embankment, where an old smokestack rose out of the pine trees. The towering cylinder was all that could be seen from their vantage of the tumbledown structure known as the Ruins, a former psychiatric hospital.

Nikki's observation had touched a nerve for both of them. Fifteen years ago, three teenagers had entered the Ruins on the night of a blood moon. One of the girls was Tom's younger sister, Ellie. It was presumed that a former mental patient known as Preacher had taken the other two girls when Tom had found Ellie the next morning facedown at the edge of the lake. He'd managed to resuscitate her, but Tom, his sister and the whole town of Belle Pointe had never been the same since that night. One of the two missing girls had turned up days later wandering down the side of a country road. The other girl had disappeared without a trace. So had Preacher.

Despite the dark history, Nikki didn't share the town's fear of the Ruins. She'd always found beauty and solace in the place, but her penchant for hanging out there when she was younger had only added fuel to the whispers of dark cults and satanic rituals after the girls had gone missing.

Tom tore his gaze from the smokestack. "Thayer's only been down here a few days, but already there's buzz about him in town. I'm surprised you haven't heard about him before now."

"I don't get out much." Nikki kept her tone neutral as she side-eyed Adam Thayer, a tall, lean man in cargo shorts, wet sneakers and a plain gray T-shirt. His hair was clipped so short that when he bent to swat a mosquito on his ankle, Nikki noticed what appeared to be a scar that ran from his forehead back into his scalp. "What's his real story?" she asked.

"Homicide detective," Tom said. "Dallas PD. Wounded in the line of duty, according to my sister. An arrest somehow turned into an ambush and shoot-out."

"That explains the scar." It was all Nikki could do to keep her gaze averted, not so much out of curiosity, but from the stranger's magnetic stare. "How does Ellie know him?"

"She went over to the Thayer house one morning to feed the peacocks and found him sitting on the front porch, drinking coffee. Evidently, he'd moved in during the night. She was wary at first, but it seems they've hit it off."

Nikki lifted a brow at his tone. "You don't approve?"

Clearly, he didn't approve.

They were still speaking in lowered voices across the body. Tom rose and moved down to the water. He motioned with a jerk of his head for Nikki to join him. She peeled off her gloves and followed him.

"Just between you and me, I plan to keep an eye on him," Tom said.

"Because of your sister?"

He hesitated. "Let's just say I don't trust anyone who feels the need to slip into town under the cover of darkness. Something odd about the way he moved in. Something odd about that shooting, too. I've got a few friends up that way. The Dallas PD kept a tight lid on the investigation. I'm not accusing him of anything, but it's a little strange that he'd relocate to a place like Belle Pointe."

Now it was Tom who'd touched a nerve. Considering that Nikki had once found herself on the wrong end of his father's unfounded suspicions, she was inclined to give Adam Thayer the benefit of the doubt. She liked Tom. He was a good man and as intuitive a law enforcement officer as she'd ever worked with, but her voice cooled just the same. "Maybe he came here to recuperate."

"And just happened upon the body of one of our most prominent citizens?"

She gave him a reproachful look. "Now who's speculating? You don't think he had anything to do with Dr. Nance's death, do you? Why would he? If he's that new in town, I doubt they even met."

"You said yourself, Dr. Nance spent a lot of time out here on the lake."

That gave her pause. "You think he saw something?"

"I think I've said too much," Tom muttered. "You're right. I'm speculating. We need to wait for the autopsy before we start drawing conclusions."

"What was odd about the shooting?" Nikki couldn't resist asking.

Tom looked troubled. "The fact that it was so thoroughly hushed up, for one thing. Hardly a mention of it in the papers or even on social media. The man took two bullets in the chest. A third skimmed his scalp. By all rights, he should be dead. He *was* dead, from what I hear. His heart stopped beating before the EMTs arrived. That kind of event involving a cop ordinarily generates more than a passing mention."

Nikki was starting to feel uneasy, too. "What are you saying, Tom?"

"Nothing. Just make sure Dr. Ramirez does a thorough job with the autopsy."

"You don't need to worry about that. He's the best there is. He knows what to look for and I'll be assisting. Two pairs of eyes, as they say. But don't expect miracles. After this long in the water..." She trailed off as she glanced out at the lake and then over her shoulder. Adam Thayer watched her with deep, brooding eyes.

Déjà vu shivered up Nikki's spine. Their paths had crossed before, she was certain. She still couldn't place him, still didn't know the why or when or how of a prior meeting. But even from a distance she could have sworn she caught the glimmer of recognition in his eyes.

The intensity of his gaze only deepened her foreboding. He was too far away to overhear their conversation, but she had a feeling he knew exactly what she was thinking. Even with state-of-the-art forensic equipment and the latest techniques, cause of death after that long in the water could be hard to prove.

No one would know that better than a homicide detective.

ADAM THAYER SLAPPED a mosquito at the back of his neck and inwardly swore. *Damn swamp.* He was being eaten alive out here. He moved into a patch of sunlight, but the bloodthirsty little bastards followed, buzzing around his ears before sinking their needles into the exposed skin at his nape.

Echo Lake was a beautiful place, a primordial paradise of sloughs, channels and open water, but the wildlife took some getting used to. He swatted and slapped and cursed some more. In the five days since he'd moved into his grandmother's old house, he'd learned to keep the bug spray handy, especially on sleepless nights when he sat out on the dock or wandered down to the bridge. Of all the days to leave home without his usual dousing.

He still didn't know what had pulled him all the way past the bridge to this particular spot. Gut instinct? The subtle waft of putrescence on the breeze?

He was no stranger to that smell. He couldn't say he missed that particular aroma or the way it sometimes lingered in the nostrils for days. But the rest of it…the methodical processing of a crime scene, the interviews, the tracking down of leads and the adrenaline rush that came with the eventual unraveling of an alibi…yeah, he missed all that. He missed his job and the way his life had been before the shooting. He missed feeling normal.

Batting away the mosquitoes, he watched the Nance County sheriff huddle with the coroner at the edge of the lake. He couldn't hear what they were saying, but he was familiar enough with death scene procedure to intuit the usual discussions about cause of death, time of death and the victim's identity.

He also knew enough about human nature to assume that his status as a material witness might soon be elevated to that of person of interest. *A stranger in town stumbles across a body, he's going to be scrutinized regardless of the circumstances.* If the sheriff suspected foul play, then said stranger would probably be questioned and maybe even surveilled if the manpower and resources could be justified.

Or maybe he was borrowing trouble. He'd been on the other side of enough interrogations to know how to handle himself. How many times had Stephanie accused him of having ice water in his veins?

Still, he didn't like the notion of being put under a microscope, his every move and utterance examined and reexamined for inconsistencies. He'd had his fill of that after the shooting. Moving into his grandmother's lake house, ostensibly to renovate and get the place ready to sell, was bound to generate talk. He'd prepared himself for a certain amount of idle curiosity and gossip. What he hadn't counted on was the sudden death of his one and only contact in town.

Shifting his position to get a better view of the body, he ignored the dull throb at his temples. Pain had become an old friend. Weeks of recovery and months of physical therapy had left a lot of jagged nerve endings. He didn't sleep much. He walked a lot and thought a lot. He pumped iron and mostly ate all the right foods. Gave up drinking. Spent time at the range. Except for the lingering headaches, he was in peak physical condition. Except for that damn psych evaluation, he would have already been reinstated. Worst mistake of his life, telling the shrink about his nightmares. Well, second worst. The first might have been trusting Stephanie.

But he couldn't go back in time. He couldn't fix all those old mistakes. He had a new concern now. Dr.

Nance was dead, which meant the old man's suspicions might have had a basis after all.

Adam's gaze moved once more to the corpse as he reflected on the conversation that had brought him to Belle Pointe. He hadn't wanted to put stock in Dr. Nance's vague misgivings, but the man could be persuasive when he wanted to be.

If you get down here and decide I'm just a delusional old coot tilting at windmills, then turn around and head back to Dallas. We'll never speak of this again. But I'm telling you, Adam. Something strange is going on in this town. Something dark. I think it has been for years.

So here he was, Adam thought. And there lay a very dead Dr. Nance.

What now?

A few hours ago, he would have liked nothing better than to pack in all the peace and quiet of the country and head straight back to the urban sprawl of his home city, a place he both loved and despised. Maybe with a little more effort, he could pick up the pieces of his shattered life. Claw his way back into the department. Maybe even give Stephanie a call.

He scowled at that thought. The chance of reconnecting with his ex-fiancée was every bit as great as the probability of his walking away from Dr. Nance's mystery, which was to say, none at all. No way he could turn his back on a dead man's last request.

As if intuiting his thoughts, the sheriff glanced over his shoulder, caught Adam's gaze and nodded briefly. Then he turned back to the coroner, speaking in low, urgent tones. She listened intently as she used the back of her gloved hand to push aside her hair.

The gesture stirred a memory. An image flitted. A vision that was there one moment and gone the next.

Who are you? Adam wondered. *How do I know you?*

He assumed a neutral expression as the sheriff pivoted away from the lake and headed up the bank toward him. The coroner returned to the victim. Two officers continued to search along the water while the remaining cops milled about in a small circle at the top of the embankment.

The young officer who had been photographing the scene joined the coroner. Navarro, the sheriff had called him earlier. He hunkered on the bank with his camera, but instead of focusing on the victim, his attention strayed to Adam. He said something to the coroner that caused her to glance over her shoulder. Her gaze met Adam's, and for a moment, he stood transfixed by the intensity of her bold stare.

Something that might have been recognition danced in her eyes, or maybe that was a glint from the dying sun. He didn't know her and yet he still had the strangest feeling that he'd seen her somewhere before. She was average height, slim build, straight dark hair pulled back and fastened haphazardly at her nape. Not beautiful by Adam's measure, but certainly attractive. A word he rarely used came to mind. *Enigmatic.*

He'd let his mind wander too far and now a piercing scream physically jolted him back to the scene. The eerie cry carried across the water and halted the sheriff in his tracks. He, along with everyone else in the area, turned anxiously toward the sound.

Everyone except the coroner. Her dark eyes remained fixed on Adam.

Chapter Two

An uneasy quiet settled over the landscape. The hair at the back of Adam's neck lifted unexpectedly as he scanned the lake. The light had dissolved rapidly with the setting sun. Twilight inched closer, deepening the sky and then the water. Still the coroner's gaze lingered.

He massaged his nape and then brushed his hand across his scalp, fingering the scar tissue that had begun to tingle. He told himself the sensation was just raw nerve endings that still needed to heal.

At the top of the embankment, someone laughed awkwardly, breaking the silence. Another officer swore. "What the hell was that?"

"A peacock," the sheriff called up to him. "Probably wandered away from the Thayer place."

"A peacock? You serious?" The officer peered across the lake. "Sounded like a woman screaming her head off to me."

Navarro crossed himself. "Maybe that's exactly what it was."

An older officer stared down at him from the top of the embankment. "The hell you talking about, son?"

Navarro's gaze swept the water. "My grandmother says this lake is haunted. She says if you come out here alone in the middle of the night, you can still hear the screams of the mental patients that were tortured in that hospital."

Someone hummed *The Twilight Zone* theme, inciting a few chuckles.

Sheriff Brannon ignored the ruckus. "Your grandmother is a fine woman, Navarro, but I wouldn't put much stock in her ghost stories."

The young officer continued undaunted. "It's not just her stories. Her cousin's friend worked in that place before the government shut it down. He said a lot of bad stuff happened there. All kinds of experiments. Things we couldn't begin to imagine. They kept the worst of the worst locked in cages on the third floor. Think of the souls that could still be trapped there." His gaze lifted to the silhouette of the smokestack.

Adam hadn't walked down to the Ruins yet, but he was itching to see the place by moonlight. Was it still there? he wondered. The secret he'd uncovered beneath the floorboards?

The prickle along his scalp intensified. He ran his fingers through his clipped hair as if he could brush away the unpleasant sensation.

The sheriff sighed wearily. "The place was shut down because funding ran out. It happened all over the country. All that talk about experiments is just an urban legend."

"Myths and legends are often based in reality," the coroner said.

Sheriff Brannon groaned. "Don't encourage him.

It was a peacock. End of story. No more talk about trapped souls and haunted lakes. We have a job to do, so let's get to it."

A muttered chorus of yessir's followed. Navarro picked up his camera. The coroner went back to her work. The deputies at the top of the embankment continued to mill about while waiting for her to release the scene. Adam gave her another quick perusal before returning his attention to the sheriff.

"You're Adam Thayer?" Tom Brannon removed his sunglasses and slipped them in his shirt pocket as he closed the distance between them. Adam was glad for that. He liked being able to see a person's eyes when he talked to him. Tom Brannon's were gray and guarded. Already a little suspicious. "My sister told me you'd moved into your grandmother's old place. Said you gave her quite a scare that first morning."

"She startled me, too. I wasn't expecting anyone to come by so early. Or at all, for that matter."

The sheriff nodded. "She promised your grandmother before she went into the hospital that she'd look after the peacocks. She's been feeding them ever since."

"Gram would appreciate that. It would have broken her heart to have them taken away."

"My sister has always had a soft spot for strays. Even the kinds that bite." His innuendo was hardly subtle. "I'm Tom Brannon, by the way."

"I know who you are." Adam's gaze dropped to the badge clipped to the man's belt. "Ellie speaks highly of you."

"That's a surprise. She tells me to my face that I'm a

pain in the ass. You know how it is with big brothers. We have a tendency to be overprotective and overbearing." His smile didn't quite reach his eyes. "You're the one who called in the body. Can you walk me through how you found him?"

"Like I told one of your officers, I'd been working inside the house all day and decided to take a walk to get some fresh air. I usually head back when I get to the bridge, but today I kept going. Needed to work out the kinks. I saw the body floating in the water, called 911 and then doubled back to wait for the first responders. I figured it would be easier if I led them back. That's when I spotted the overturned fishing boat wedged up against the bridge supports. It wasn't noticeable from the other direction. I waded out to make sure no one was trapped underneath and then I climbed up to the road when I heard the sirens."

The sheriff took all that in without comment. "Your grandmother's house is on the water. Have you noticed any unusual activity on the lake since you've been here?"

"I don't know about unusual. I sometimes hear boats at all hours. Night fishing must be pretty popular around here."

The sheriff's expression turned glum. "Among other activities. You've been here, what? Close to a week?" He gave a quick nod toward the body. "You ever see that man on the water? Or maybe on one of your walks? He had a fishing cabin across the lake from your grandmother's house. He may have been staying there before he died."

"I never saw him there."

The sheriff gave him a shrewd appraisal. "You sure? He's not that easy to recognize in his current state."

Adam squinted into a patch of dying sunlight. "I'm sure I would have recognized Dr. Nance if I'd seen him on the water or anywhere else."

Brannon stared at him for another long moment. He didn't seem surprised by the revelation, though it was unlikely he knew about Adam's friendship with the dead man. He couldn't have known about that last phone call, either, unless Dr. Nance had gone to him for help. Given that possibility, Adam decided not to hold anything back. Information had a way of coming out, and the last thing he needed was to have the local authorities turn on him, too.

"You might have mentioned earlier that you knew him," Brannon said.

Adam shrugged. "I had no idea who the victim was until you turned him over. Even then, I wasn't certain until I heard you say his name."

Brannon accepted the explanation with a vague nod. "How did you know him?"

"He was my grandmother's doctor for years. She thought the world of him."

"Everyone did. He was one of a kind. He'll be sorely missed around here."

Did he detect a hint of accusation in the sheriff's tone or was he being paranoid? Adam wondered.

"I can understand why," he said. "When my grandmother took a bad turn, my dad had her transferred to a facility in Dallas. Dr. Nance still came to see her as often as he could. He and I became acquainted during his visits. We were both with her at the end. His kindness made an impression. You don't often see that side of human nature in our line of work."

Brannon's gaze flicked to the scar on Adam's scalp. "Ellie tells me you were a detective."

"I still am, Sheriff."

He looked unimpressed by the clarification. "She said you were wounded in the line of duty. Said you almost died."

Adam hesitated. He would share what he knew about Dr. Nance, but he had no intention of elaborating on his own injuries or the fallout from the shooting. That was private business. He'd told Ellie Brannon enough to quell any misgivings she might have about her new neighbor, but he'd kept the really dark stuff to himself. The threats and suspicions. Stephanie's betrayal. The underlying politics involved in his delayed reinstatement.

"I don't like to talk about it," he said. "You can understand that, having been through a similar event yourself recently."

A frown flickered. "Ellie told you about that?"

"She said you'd been shot. She didn't supply the details and I didn't ask for any. That's your business. What happened in Dallas is my business. It has nothing to do with Dr. Nance's death."

"Maybe not, but I can't help wondering what brings someone like you to Belle Pointe. We're not exactly on the beaten path. Why now when your grandmother's house has sat empty for so long?" He glanced over his shoulder at the body. "Under the circumstances, you can understand why I might find your timing a little curious."

Tom Brannon was nobody's fool. Adam warned himself to tread carefully with this guy.

"The timing isn't coincidental," he admitted. "I came because Dr. Nance asked me to."

"He asked you to come to Belle Pointe? Why?"

"He said something strange was going on down here. Something dark. His words exactly."

The sheriff looked momentarily startled. "What did he mean by that?"

"I don't know. He wouldn't talk about it over the phone. I suggested he come to you with his concerns, but he said he didn't want to embarrass himself or waste your time until he knew for certain he wasn't imagining things. He asked me to come down, take a look at what he'd found and make sure he wasn't going crazy. Also his words."

The sheriff canted his head as he considered everything Adam had told him. "When was this?"

"He called early last week. Tuesday, I think. I owed him a favor, so I agreed to come."

"Just like that." There was that note of suspicion again.

Adam shrugged. "More or less."

The sheriff said pensively, "Ellie said you arrived on Sunday of this week. Today is Thursday. I'm guessing he's been in the water longer than five days. Weren't you concerned when you arrived and didn't hear from him?"

"He told me he'd be out of town for a few days. A medical conference in Houston, I think. I decided to come down early and get settled in. I wasn't sure my grandmother's house would even be livable. So, no, I wasn't concerned when he didn't call."

Brannon's expression turned grim. "He obviously didn't make it to that conference. Why do you suppose he didn't tell anyone about his change of plans? Is it possible he drove out to the lake to see you?"

The throbbing intensified at Adam's temples. He resisted the urge to press his thumbs to the pulse points. "I doubt it. He didn't know I would be arriving early. It was a spur-of-the-moment decision."

Brannon fell silent. Adam could well imagine all the scenarios churning inside his head, all the loose threads and unanswered questions that would keep him awake that night. When the sheriff finally spoke, something new had crept into his voice. "How did he seem when you last talked to him?"

Adam said carefully, "If you're asking about his mental state, the only thing I can tell you is that he didn't seem himself. At least, not the Dr. Nance I knew. He sounded anxious and paranoid. He was sometimes distracted. Frankly, that's another reason I agreed to come. I was afraid he might be losing it. He sounded as if he might be worried about that, too."

Brannon turned to skim the lake, letting his gaze drift toward the bridge. For a moment, he seemed to forget Adam's presence. "The onset of dementia would be hard for a man of his intellect and accomplishment to accept."

"It would be hard for anyone to accept," Adam said. "Are you suggesting he deliberately crashed his boat into those pilings?"

The sheriff frowned. "I'm not suggesting anything. Just thinking out loud."

"Is there any reason to suspect foul play?"

The interview had shifted and Brannon didn't like it. His scowl deepened as he returned his focus to Adam. "I'm not going to stand here and speculate about cause of death," he said in a brusque tone. "That determination will be made by Dr. Dresden and her colleagues at the lab."

"Dr. Dresden?" The name zinged along Adam's scalp like an electrical shock. *Dresden. Dresden.* How did he know that name?

"Nikki Dresden. The Nance County coroner."

Adam's gaze shot across the bank to where she knelt beside the body.

Nikki Dresden. Holy hell. Now he remembered where their paths had crossed. Now he understood his strong reaction to her.

She looked very different from the last time Adam had seen her, but then, people changed in fifteen years. People grew up. Most people, anyway. He certainly wasn't the same person he'd been at seventeen. Nikki Dresden had undergone a dramatic transformation in both appearance and stature. Adam would never have placed her if he hadn't heard her name, but he supposed that was understandable. They hadn't been friends or even acquaintances. He doubted they'd exchanged more than a dozen words during the entire summer he'd spent with his grandmother. Still, as odd as it now seemed, there'd been a time when he felt he knew Nikki Dresden better than he knew himself.

He scanned her features, searching for even a shadow

of the eccentric girl he remembered. Gone were the black clothes, the dyed hair and the mask of heavy makeup. Her hair was still dark, but natural and glossy, her face scrubbed clean of cosmetics. She looked intense, yet comfortable in her skin and confident in her element. She had her kit open beside the body as she gathered samples, her brow furrowed in concentration. She didn't look up from her work, but Adam had a funny feeling she was all too aware of his interest.

He watched her for a moment longer before the sheriff once again commanded his attention.

"I take it you'll be sticking around for a while," Brannon said.

"I don't have a timetable." Adam ran a hand over his head as he averted his gaze from the coroner. "There's a lot to be done at my grandmother's place."

"Good luck with that. In the meantime, I'd like you to leave a contact number. Depending on the autopsy results, I may need you to come in and give a statement." Adam supplied his phone number and the sheriff jotted it in his notebook. "I'll be in touch. You're free to go, but I'd appreciate your discretion until we can make the official notifications."

Adam nodded his agreement and then moved away from the perimeter, stepping deeper into the shade of the pine forest before pausing to glance back. Between his prickling scar and throbbing temples, he felt as if the top of his head might come off. Maybe he wasn't as healed as he wanted to believe. Maybe his peak physical condition was only an illusion or wishful thinking. *Maybe* he would never be the same man he'd been before the shooting.

He didn't want to think about that. Easier to drift back into the past than to worry about his uncertain future. Besides, the coroner's transformation fascinated him.

"Nikki Dresden." Her name slipped out on a whisper, barely audible even to his own ears, but the wind seemed to tear it from his lips and carry it down to the edge of the water. No way she could have heard him, yet her head came up and she searched the tree line until she found him.

Their gazes locked for the longest moment. The charged tingle at his scalp raced all the way down to his fingertips. She felt it, too. He could have sworn he saw again the glint of recognition in her dark eyes and maybe this time a hint of fear.

With good reason.

I know who you are, Nikki Dresden. I know what you did that summer.

Chapter Three

Dusk had fallen in earnest by the time the stretcher arrived. The horizon deepened from scarlet to violet and
the moon was just starting to shimmer through the pine
trees. A mild breeze drifted off the water, but the air
was still hot and humid and the drone of mosquitoes
seemed incessant.

Nikki oversaw the removal of the body and then
waited until the last squad car had pulled away from
the side of the road before she climbed up to her vehicle and changed out of the damp coveralls into fresh
clothes and dry sneakers. Then she traipsed back down
to the lake. She had one last thing she wanted to do
before heading home.

Turning her back on the bridge, she hurried past
the spot where the body had been recovered and then
moved steadily along the bank until the path ended
at a steep embankment. She could just make out the
roofline and the smokestack that rose from the boiler
room at the back of the property. She'd been called out
to the Ruins recently when another body had been discovered at the bottom of an old elevator shaft. That trip
had brought back a lot of memories for Nikki. She'd

been meaning to return sooner, but one thing after another had kept her away.

When she was a kid, she'd considered the Ruins her own private hideaway. She'd spent a lot of time prowling through the maze of hallways and rooms. Despite the dark history, she'd never felt uneasy or oppressed there, never felt lonely in that abandoned place when all she'd ever felt at home or in school was alone.

After Riley Cavanaugh had gone missing, Nikki's trips dwindled, not because she was afraid of being taken, but because her visits had started to feel intrusive, like she was violating a sacred place.

Using vines for leverage, she scrambled up the embankment and paused at the top to scour the looming facade. Most of the windows were broken and a part of the roof had caved in. Curling tentacles of ivy grew up the brick face, reaching for the eaves and creeping through shattered windowpanes. Ignoring the decay, Nikki trailed her gaze over the graceful arches and stately pillars and thought again what a beautiful place it must once have been.

She entered through one of the arches, using her flashlight to chase away shadows from all the deep corners. Running the light up one wall and across the ceiling, she paused on the demonic mural that someone had painted of Preacher. Red eyes stared down at her. Had he really taken Riley Cavanaugh? No one knew for certain. They might never know. The mystery of her disappearance still haunted the town—still haunted Nikki—fifteen years later.

Moving away from the mural, she made her way up two sets of precarious stairs to the third floor. The tall, arched window at the end of the hallway allowed in sunlight by day and moonlight by night. Nikki kept her gaze averted from the area at the back of the building. She didn't want to think about the poor, damaged souls who had once been locked up there.

She found *her* room and entered cautiously, wary of the sloping floor and sagging ceiling tiles. Nothing remained of the original furnishings. Most of the beds and mattresses had either been carted away years ago or piled in the basement for rats to nest in. The iron bars at the windows had been removed and sold for scrap metal. Graffiti covered the peeling walls, some of it strange and disturbing, some of it quite beautiful.

Nikki crossed the floor, pausing over a loose board that creaked beneath her weight. She resisted the urge to drop to her knees and pry it loose. Maybe she would before she left. Wasn't that why she'd come? To retrieve a part of her past she'd left hidden here all those years ago?

She'd been wondering ever since her last visit to the Ruins if the journal was still there. All those dark secrets and breathless confessions she'd poured onto the pages of a spiral notebook. Or had rodents chewed away at her teenage angst, leaving nothing behind but the metal binding?

Nikki had abandoned the journal and her all-black wardrobe when she left Belle Pointe for college. She'd wanted a fresh start in Austin. No sense dragging that baggage with her. But it was hard to bury one's past completely. She was older now, and age put a lot of things into perspective. Maybe she would find it cathartic to revisit the weird, dramatic girl she'd once been.

Right now, though, she needed a few minutes in this quiet place to think about Dr. Nance.

Hoisting herself up to the window ledge, she sat with legs dangling as she gazed out at the water. The rising moon seemed to hover over his fishing cabin, as if the whole universe mourned his passing.

Why had he gone out to the lake when he was supposed to be in Houston? Why hadn't he told anyone about his change of plans? How did a strong swimmer such as he was end up floating facedown in the water?

Accidents happened. Nikki saw the results of carelessness and happenstance every day, and yet doubts continued to plague her. She hoped the autopsy would provide answers, but after so many days in the water, the breakdown of organs and soft tissue could make a definitive conclusion impossible. The diagnosis would likely come down to a matter of elimination and educated guesswork.

A floorboard groaned out in the hallway, and Nikki whirled, catching a glimpse of a silhouette through the doorway. Startled, she swung her legs inside and grabbed the flashlight as she hopped down from the ledge. "Who's there?"

A deep voice said from the shadows, "Adam Thayer. Sorry. I didn't mean to scare you. I didn't know anyone would be up here."

Really? He just happened to come up to the third floor, to the very room Nikki had always claimed as her domain?

"What are you doing here?"

"Exploring." He appeared in the doorway then, a tall, lean figure with eyes that seemed to pierce through the gloom until he found her. "It's Dr. Dresden, isn't it? I saw you on the bank earlier."

Nikki gripped the flashlight. Why she felt threatened by Adam Thayer, she didn't know, but that niggling familiarity unsettled her. "Yes, I saw you down there, too. You're the one who found Dr. Nance's body."

He remained on the threshold as he took a quick survey of their surroundings. Was he noting how alone they were? How isolated this place was? Nikki didn't want to be that person who eyed a stranger in town with unwarranted suspicion, but neither could she ignore the little voice in her head that told her to tread carefully with this man.

"I saw the vehicles drive off a little while ago," he said. "I would have thought you'd left with the others."

I should have. I really, really should have. "I needed some time to think," she said with an uneasy shrug. "I've always found this place peaceful."

"*This* place?"

Strangely, his incredulity relaxed her a little. She allowed a slight smile. "I guess that does sound strange, considering."

He ran a hand through his clipped hair as he glanced around. "No, I get it. I think. If you want peace and quiet, you can't get much more secluded than this. The view of the lake from that window is killer." He paused. "Mind if I take a closer look?"

She stepped away, keeping him in her line of sight and the doorway in her periphery.

He walked across the room, testing—she could have sworn—the loose floorboard she'd noted earlier. But his hesitation was undoubtedly her imagination.

Propping his hands on the ledge, he leaned out into the breeze. Nikki studied his profile. He looked tall and lean and dangerous in the gathering darkness. Déjà vu taunted, prickling her spine and lifting the hair at the back of her neck.

Who are you, Adam Thayer?

"I can see my grandmother's house from here." His voice was a deep, rich baritone. The low timbre seemed intimate in the quiet room.

"In the winter after the leaves have fallen, you can see all the way across the state line into Louisiana," Nikki told him.

He pulled back to glance at her in the shadows. "You come out here a lot, I take it."

"I used to. Not so much anymore." She surprised herself by moving up beside him and leaning into the breeze. The air had finally cooled and the lake looked soft and shimmery under a full moon. "When I was a kid, I could spend hours sitting in this window reading or just staring out at the lake. It was my favorite place in the whole world, though granted, my world was pretty limited back then." She closed her eyes for a moment, letting the scent of honeysuckle and old memories whisper over her.

"You weren't afraid of all those trapped souls?"

The teasing quality in his voice made her warm to him, but she didn't want to warm to Adam Thayer. She didn't want to feel anything for him tonight or ever. "I was never afraid here. There are far, far scarier things than ghosts." Her gaze lifted to the scar at his scalp. "You probably know that better than I do."

"I'm betting we've both seen our share of horror

stories." He turned, propping his shoulder against the window frame as he gazed at her in the thin light. "It's always hard when the victim is someone you know." A slight pause. "You and Dr. Nance were close?"

"He was a mentor and a dear friend." She was amazed at how unemotional she sounded when tears burned behind her eyelids.

He folded his arms, seemingly at ease. "I got to know him pretty well before my grandmother passed away. He spoke often about someone he called Nik. He never mentioned a last name, only that you were a doctor. He was very proud of you."

Nikki cleared her throat. "He was a very special person."

"Yes. That was the impression I had of him." Adam turned back to the window, staring out into the night with a brooding frown. "What do you think happened? The overturned boat would suggest an accidental drowning, but things aren't always what they seem."

Nikki struggled to keep her voice dispassionate. "I don't like to speculate. Hopefully, the autopsy will give us some answers."

"Do you really think it will, though? After that long in the water?"

"We have one of the finest forensic pathologists in the state on our team. If there's anything to find, Dr. Ramirez will find it."

"That's good to know." He pressed fingertips to his temples as he closed his eyes briefly. Nikki thought again about the shooting, about Tom Brannon's suspicions. About how easily she'd leaped to a stranger's defense because of her past experiences with Tom's father.

She liked to keep an open mind, but there were times when it paid to be cautious.

"Are you all right?" she couldn't help asking.

He dropped his hands to the ledge without answering. "If I were you, I'd pay close attention to the toxicology screen. Minute traces of toxins can go undetected in cases where cause of death is presumed accidental."

Nikki bristled. "I don't presume anything. Contrary to what you seem to think, we know what we're doing down here."

"I didn't mean to imply otherwise."

"Sure you did."

"If that's how I came across, I apologize. I'm not trying to step on any toes, but I do have a vested interest in this case. I'm here because Dr. Nance asked me to come."

Nikki grudgingly accepted his apology with a brief nod. "Sheriff Brannon mentioned that Dr. Nance had called you recently."

"We talked early last week. He told me something strange was going on in Belle Pointe. Something dark. That it probably had been for years."

"It?"

"He wouldn't elaborate. When I pressed him, he said he'd tell me everything when I got here. He mentioned something about files and notes. He said it was all there in black and white, but he wanted me to come down and help him make sense of it. And to make sure he wasn't going crazy."

Nikki's voice sharpened. "He said that to you? He was that worried about his mental state?"

"Apparently."

She said pensively, "This talk about something strange and dark going on in Belle Pointe... Would you say he sounded delusional?"

"I don't know if I'd go that far. I can tell you this. He didn't sound like the Dr. Nance I'd come to know." His gaze narrowed, as if he were trying to recall the nuances of that phone call. "Are you aware of any medication he was taking?"

"I never knew him to take so much as an over-the-counter pain reliever," Nikki said. "However, we'll request his medical records before the autopsy. That's procedure. But even with a full history at our disposal, cause of death remains indeterminate in more cases than most people realize."

"One step at a time," Adam said.

She nodded, shifting her gaze from the lake to his profile and then back to the water. Recognition still tugged and a memory flitted, lingering in the light for only a moment before skittering back to the fringes of her subconscious. Nikki suddenly had an almost overwhelming sense of fate and she didn't know why.

Beside her, Adam stirred. "I should go and let you get back to your solitude."

"No, wait. I need to ask you something first."

He stared down at her for the longest moment before he nodded. Nikki couldn't tell what color his eyes were, only that they were dark like hers, but with a golden shimmer. Or was that the moonlight playing tricks?

He leaned an elbow against the ledge and waited.

"This may sound like a very bad cliché," she said tentatively. "But I have a feeling we've met before. You seem so familiar to me and yet I can't place you at all. It's been bugging me ever since I saw you at the lake earlier."

"It took me a while to figure it out, too."

Her breath caught. "Then we have met. When? Where?"

"Right here."

"Here? At the Ruins, you mean?" Her heart thudded as her focus plunged momentarily to the loose floorboard at their feet. He couldn't know. No one knew. She'd never told anyone about her secret hiding place. Never confessed to anyone what she'd done.

And yet…the way he stared down at her in the dark…the way his voice lowered knowingly…

She suppressed a shiver. "I'm sorry. I still don't remember."

"It was the summer that local girl went missing. Riley Cavanaugh." His deep gaze took her in. "Surely you remember her."

ADAM SEARCHED HER face in the moonlight. She didn't react to the name, but he could sense her wariness. The tension in the room thickened oppressively.

Something crept into her voice that he couldn't identify. "Of course I remember Riley. Everyone in town remembers Riley Cavanaugh. But I still can't place you. Are you sure we met *here*?"

"We never actually met," he said. "I saw you out here with your friends from time to time, but mostly you came alone. Your nose was usually buried in a book or else you were scribbling in a notebook. We spoke only once that I recall. You made it clear you didn't like to be bothered, so I kept my distance."

She shook her head helplessly.

Adam didn't know whether to be amused or insulted that someone had blocked a memory of him so thoroughly. In Dallas, he had people come up to him on a regular basis to either thank or berate him for a previous interaction. To Nikki Dresden, he was a complete nonentity.

But she was still trying. He'd give her that.

"Who were your friends?" she asked. "Did you hang out with any of the local kids?"

"I didn't socialize much that summer. I was sent down here to work."

"Where did you work?" Before he could answer, she rushed to add, "I'm sorry. I don't mean to sound as if I'm interrogating you. I just know it'll drive me crazy until I can put a memory with your face."

"It's okay. It'll come back to you eventually." Or maybe it wouldn't. And maybe that would be for the best. He'd probably stayed too long in her orbit as it was. The last thing he needed was an entanglement, no matter how superficial or fleeting. Stephanie's betrayal was still too raw and he was in no hurry to go down that road again. Nikki Dresden fascinated him and that was never a good sign.

"I worked for my grandmother," he said. "I'd just graduated high school and made the mistake of telling my folks I had no intention of going to college in the fall. So my dad sent me down here to repair some storm damage to my grandmother's roof and dock. He figured a few weeks of working in the hot sun might persuade me to reevaluate my options."

"Did it?"

"You could say that. By the end of the summer, I went back home determined to become a police detective."

She glanced up at him. "That seems an odd transition."

He didn't know how long she expected him to keep talking, but she seemed in no hurry to end the conversation. So he settled in and returned her curious stare. "Like I said. That was the summer Riley Cavanaugh went missing."

A long pause.

She tore her gaze from his and glanced back out at the lake. "Did you know Riley?"

"No."

"But you decided to become a police detective because of her disappearance?"

"That was the catalyst."

"Strange."

They both fell silent, each lost in thought as night sounds drifted in through the open window. Adam studied her profile from his periphery. She was a coroner, but he didn't see death when he looked at her—the opposite, in fact. Youth and vitality radiated from her slender form like heat waves shimmering off asphalt. She wasn't beautiful like Stephanie, but she was far more attractive than he'd given her credit for earlier. And still just as enigmatic.

"Tell me more about your summer here," she said. "We were all so close to what happened. Riley's disappearance affected everyone who knew her in one way or another. It's interesting to hear an outside perspective."

"Haven't I taken up enough of your time?"

"No, please. Go on."

He shrugged. "It was a long time ago. A lot's happened since then. But I remember when I first got to town that the other girl had just been found wandering down a rural road."

"Jenna Malloy."

"Yes, Jenna. She was in such a state she couldn't tell the police anything about their abductor or what had happened to them. Her trauma and Riley's disappearance were all anyone could talk about, including my grandmother. Before long, I became caught up in the mystery, too. At some point, I got it in my head that I could do what the local police, the county sheriff's office, the Texas Rangers and the FBI couldn't. Find Riley Cavanaugh."

The note of self-deprecation in his voice didn't seem to register with Nikki. Resting her head against the window frame, she lifted a hand to tuck back the loose strands of hair at her temple. "Everyone looked for Riley. The search went on for months. They brought in bloodhounds, psychics. No one could find her." She shook her head sadly. "It was a terrible time for her family. For the whole town. I don't think Belle Pointe ever recovered."

"Something like that changes a community," Adam said. "Especially if there's never an arrest. People get suspicious of one another. Rumors start circulating."

"Oh, there were plenty of rumors."

"People like to talk," he agreed. "The consensus seemed to be that the abductor was a former psychiatric patient named Silas Creed. Preacher, they called him, because of the fiery sermons he delivered on the front steps after this place was closed down. You said you spent a lot of time here as a kid. Did you ever see him?"

She shook her head. "Not here. Not that I remember. But I saw him around town now and then. He did odd jobs to get by. My grandmother always warned me to keep my distance, but before the disappearances, he just seemed like a harmless outcast to me. I felt sorry for him."

"Do you think he did it?"

"I don't know. No one ever saw him again after that night. The way he skipped town certainly seemed suspicious. But I always wondered if he ran away because he was afraid of being blamed. People tend to scapegoat those who are different."

Adam's voice softened. "He wasn't the only scapegoat in Belle Pointe, was he?"

"No." She lifted her face to the sky. Her skin looked pale and translucent in the moonlight, her eyes dark and unfathomable. Something stirred inside Adam. Something unexpected and completely unwise. Maybe even dangerous, considering the circumstances.

"You looked a lot different back then," he said.

"Which is why my friends and I were scapegoated." She scowled into the night. "If you were around that summer, you must have heard those rumors, too."

"About satanic cults and devil worshipping? Yeah."

She gave him a sidelong glance. "You aren't afraid to be alone with me out here?"

"Not for a second."

His conviction seemed to rattle her. "Maybe you should be."

He pointed to the scar at his scalp. "Foolish or not, I'm not that easily spooked."

She turned back to the lake. "The police targeted us because of the way we dressed, the books we read, the music we listened to. People started calling us the Belle Pointe Five." She shrugged, though it was obvious the memory still stung. "Small towns can be rife with narrow minds."

"The city, as well," he said. "For what it's worth, I never believed those rumors."

"Why not? You didn't know me."

Because I found your journal beneath that loose floorboard. Because I learned from reading your innermost secrets that you and your friends were also harmless outcasts.

Harmless…but not altogether innocent.

"I wanted to form my own opinion about what happened," he said carefully. "In my spare time, I scoured online news sites and social media for accounts of the disappearances, gathering whatever bits of information I could find. It was like putting together a puzzle. I dug it. After pounding nails all day in the hot sun, I'd sometimes take a dip in the lake and then hike down here to poke through the rubble, hoping to uncover something that had been missed by the local authorities."

"Did you?"

A loaded question.

He hesitated. "Nothing that would lead me to Riley Cavanaugh."

She fell silent once more, leaning through the window into the breeze. The reflection of the moon on the lake was magnetic, drawing Adam's gaze down into those dark, murky depths. All their talk about an old disappearance had made him momentarily forget why he was really here. *Something strange is going on in this town. Something dark. I think it has been for years.*

"Someone's down there," Nikki said.

The comment startled him out of a deep reverie. "What? Where?"

She pointed toward the bank. "He's there, just beyond that large cypress tree. You can barely make out a silhouette. I've been watching him for the past minute or so. I thought it was a bush or a limb at first. But then I saw him move down toward the water. Now he's just hunkered there behind that tree as if he's waiting for something."

"Could he be fishing?" Adam peered through the darkness, trailing his gaze slowly along the bank, then darting back when he spotted the silhouette.

"Whoever he is, I doubt he's fishing," Nikki murmured. "I never heard a boat. He must have walked down from the bridge."

He was too far away and it was too dark out even with the full moon to tell who he was or what he might be up to. For all they knew, the man could have a perfectly innocent reason for sitting in the shadows staring out at the lake. But he wasn't that far from where Dr. Nance's body had been recovered. That and his stealthy behavior triggered Adam's wariness.

"Do you think he heard about Dr. Nance?" Nikki asked. "Maybe he came out here to see where it happened."

"Like one of the creeps who shows up at crime and accident scenes out of morbid curiosity?"

"It would explain why he's just sitting there," she mused.

Adam turned on his flashlight and shone it down toward the water.

The beam wasn't bright enough to penetrate all the way down to the bank, but it got the person's attention. Instead of running away, he turned on a spotlight and directed the beam up to the very window where they stood.

"Damn." Adam turned off his flashlight and motioned for Nikki to move back from the window.

She eased into the shadows as her breath quickened. "What do you think he's doing?"

"No idea." Adam kept to the side of the window as he glanced out. "But that's a powerful light to lug around for some random weirdo looking for a death scene."

His face looked suddenly threatening in the moonlight and his whole body seemed to tense. Nikki had worked closely with law enforcement her entire career. She was in her element around most cops, but there was something about Adam Thayer that continued to unnerve her. It wasn't just the fact that she couldn't place him or even the way he looked at her. The man obviously had secrets. What had really happened to him in Dallas and why was Tom Brannon so suspicious of that shooting? Was he that protective of his sister or had he picked up the same uneasy vibe that now trickled down Nikki's backbone, forming an icy knot at the base of her spine?

She said nervously, "People use spotlights all the time on the lake. Sometimes logs float just beneath the surface. Not to mention all the other hidden debris in the water that can bend a prop or puncture a fiberglass hull."

"As you pointed out, he's not in a boat." Adam left the window and crossed the room to check the hallway.

Nikki turned to track him. "What are you doing? Did you hear something?"

"No. Just making sure." He glanced both ways down the corridor before turning back into the room.

Nikki watched him in the moonlight. That sense of fate kept tugging, making her self-conscious of his nearness and too hypersensitive to the doubts that Tom Brannon had voiced about him earlier.

"Maybe he's waiting for a drug deal to go down," she said in a hushed voice. "There's a big meth and fentanyl problem in this county." The spotlight went off and the room once again fell into darkness. Adam eased back up to the window. Nikki moved to the other side. "Can you still see him?"

"No. He may have taken off when he realized he wasn't alone."

She peered out into the darkness. "You don't think he'd come up here, do you? He obviously saw your light."

"I doubt it, but I'll go down and check things out. You stay here and keep watch."

She shot him a worried look. "Do you think that's wise? If a drug deal is in progress, there'll be others out there or on their way. Those people don't mess around. I've seen their handiwork."

"I'll be fine. Keep your eyes peeled, but stay out of sight. Let me know if you spot anything out of the ordinary."

"What's out of the ordinary?" Nikki muttered.

"Any suspicious movement."

"I'm assuming you don't want me to shout a warning out the window," she said.

"Good point."

They exchanged phones, entered their numbers and then swapped back. Adam took another look out the window before he disappeared into the hallway. Nikki remained on guard, her attention riveted along the bank as she listened to the creaking floorboards in the corridor and the soft thud of retreating footsteps on the stairs.

A few moments later, Adam exited the building and made his way through the weeds to the top of the embankment. He started down without a backward glance and was soon lost to her view. She picked him up again when he got to the bottom and headed along the bank. He moved quickly, using shadows and trees for cover. Nikki swept the area, but detected no other movement. The night seemed very still all of a sudden. Even the breeze had died away.

He left the trail and headed into the woods. Nikki watched and waited, her muscles taut with tension. What an evening this had turned out to be. She'd barely had time to process Dr. Nance's death, much less to grieve. Maybe it was better this way. Time enough later to plunge down that dark rabbit hole. She knew from past experience it would be no easy feat to crawl back out. She preferred to drift a little longer in shock and disbelief.

After a bit, her phone pinged and she glanced at the screen.

All clear. Don't see anyone around.

She texted back: Are you coming back up?

Headed that way now.

She pocketed the phone and watched until she knew the coast was clear before she left her position at the window. Locating the loose floorboard, she knelt and used the blade of her grandfather's Swiss Army knife to pry up the edge so that she could slip the board from the groove. Then she shone her flashlight down into the space. Cobwebs shimmered. Brushing aside the sticky threads, she reached into the cubby, feeling all along the bottom for the tattered edges of her journal.

The notebook was gone. All her secrets were gone.

Sitting back on her heels, she stared at the empty space for a moment before she finally rose and moved back to the window. She couldn't see Adam. He was probably already climbing up the embankment. He would remain invisible until he reached the top. She could picture him out there now, scaling the steep slope in a few long strides. He wouldn't need vines to pull himself up. He wouldn't slip and slide and clutch at dead branches the way Nikki had.

Dropping once more to the floor, she flattened herself facedown so she could reach deeper into the niche. Her fingertips touched a smooth surface. Whatever was in there had been pushed back just beyond her reach.

She pressed her cheek to the floor and angled the flashlight beam into the cavity. Something gold glinted.

Stretching as far as she could reach, she managed to scoot the object toward her until she could wrap her fingers around it. A moment later, she removed a green wooden box with a small gold crown on the top.

She blew dust from the lid and then opened it. The watch inside was large, iconic, and looked to be solid gold. Carefully, she removed the band from the holder and held the crystal face up to the light. Her heart hammered by this time and a cold sweat beaded on her forehead. Still hunkering next to the hidey-hole, she turned over the watch, focusing the flashlight beam on the back of the case until she could make out the engraved initials: C.N.

Charles Nance.

Nikki had never seen Dr. Nance wear this particular watch—he preferred a more practical timepiece for everyday use—but she had no doubt it was his. The expensive watch had been a gift from his late wife, Audrey, and he only wore it on special occasions. When not in use, it remained safely tucked away in the green box and was given a place of honor on the fireplace mantel in Dr. Nance's study, along with a framed wedding photograph of his beloved wife. Nikki only knew about the gift and its history because Dr. Nance's housekeeper, Dessie Dupre, had once given her a peek when Nikki had helped dust Dr. Nance's study. The shrine of items had fascinated Nikki, so Dessie had carefully removed the box from the mantel and opened the lid with reverence.

She was already dying when she gave it to him, poor thing. Now he wears it every year on their anniversary. That's how special it is to him. The rest of the time it sits right here in this pretty green box.

Is it gold, Miss Dessie?

Solid gold, child. Worth a pretty penny, too. But you can't put a price tag on a memory like that.

So how had Dr. Nance's gold watch ended up in Nikki's secret hiding place?

Someone had put it there some time ago, judging by the thick layer of dust on the box and the undisturbed cobwebs in the cubby.

The same someone who had removed her journal?

Chapter Four

The watch was a puzzle, seemingly unconnected to Dr. Nance's death, if one believed in coincidences. Nikki wasn't sure that she did, but she also couldn't deny the evidence of dust and cobwebs that suggested the box had been placed beneath the floorboard long before Dr. Nance had died.

She fretted about that watch and her missing journal as she lay in bed that night, unable to sleep. She thought about Dr. Nance all alone on the lake, realizing he was in trouble but powerless to save himself. Had she missed an important clue the last time she spoke with him? Had he been distracted and paranoid, perhaps even delusional, and she'd been too caught up in her own life to even notice?

After everything he'd done for her, Nikki hated to think that she'd let him down when he'd needed her most, that he had turned to a stranger for help instead of her. But then, Adam Thayer hadn't been a stranger to Dr. Nance. Maybe not to her, either, if she could just place him.

As she was dozing off, recognition finally came to her. She almost bolted upright at the memory.

It hadn't been at the Ruins after all. Not her first glimpse of him. She'd spied him on the bridge one day as she trudged down from the road. She hadn't known his name then, but she could tell even from a distance that he was one of *them*. Those popular, privileged few who seemed to glide through life bathed in a golden light.

Bronzed and broad-shouldered, skin glistening in the hot sun, he'd hovered at the very edge of the bridge deck before executing a near-perfect backflip into the water. Hidden by the lush vegetation on the embankment, Nikki had watched from afar, fascinated by the stranger in spite of herself.

He'd looked very different back then, too. His hair had been long enough to touch his shoulders, dark, thick and carelessly tousled. Nikki remembered the way he had come up out of the water, slinging droplets from that glorious mop before striking out for the bank.

His clipped hair now revealed too much. Not just the scar across his scalp, but the lines of pain around his mouth and the deep shadows of distrust and cynicism in his eyes. Those shadows made Nikki wonder again about the shooting, about his past.

The image of a young Adam Thayer kept her awake for a very long time. Her alarm roused her at seven with a shrill jolt. Exhausted, she dragged herself out of bed and gulped coffee on her way to the lab.

Like every day, she spent the morning performing autopsies, and then she and her colleagues convened in the consultation room after lunch to go over the results. Fridays were always a rush, and normally, Dr. Nance's autopsy would have been pushed to Monday since the Northeast Texas Forensic Science Center was closed on weekends, but Dr. Ramirez had agreed to come in early the next day. Nikki was grateful. The sooner they had answers, the better.

As busy as her morning was, she managed to squeeze in a call to Tom Brannon. He'd come back out to the Ruins the night before to take possession of the watch, bagging and tagging both the timepiece and the green box into evidence. Then early this morning he'd driven over to Dr. Nance's house to confirm ownership with Dessie Dupre.

According to Dessie, the watch had been missing for years. Dr. Nance had assumed a worker who'd had access to the house had taken it, though nothing had ever been proved. The theft had been reported to the local police department, but the culprit was never found. That was all Dessie could tell him about the watch, Tom said. She'd been too upset by news of Dr. Nance's death to be of much help otherwise.

He and Nikki spoke for a few more minutes and then she went back to work.

By the time she finally drove home, twilight had fallen and a few stars twinkled out. She parked in the garage and went through the side door into the backyard. A mild breeze stirred the wind chimes that hung from a tree branch, and she paused at the bottom of the back steps to enjoy the evening air.

The former owner of the property had been an avid gardener, and every day when Nikki got home from work, she tried to take a few moments to savor the fruits of her predecessor's labors. The roses that grew next to the house were especially fragrant in the breeze and she closed her eyes as she drew in the heady aroma.

Tonight more than ever she was thankful for her little sanctuary. In her line of work, it was important to have a quiet place where she could unwind at the end of the day. She'd learned a long time ago how to compartmentalize, but she was vulnerable in her grief and unwanted memories came calling, threatening to lure her back into the gloomy despair of her youth.

She'd come a long way since those miserable days, in no small part because of Dr. Nance's guidance and encouragement. He'd be the last person who'd want her to wallow. She could almost hear him scolding her in that teasing, pragmatic way he had. *Life is for the living, Nik. Say your goodbyes and get on with it.*

Easier said than done, of course. Her personal loss aside, as the Nance County coroner, she still had too many questions about his death.

A bat swooped low, drawing her attention skyward. She watched the dusky horizon for a moment longer before climbing the steps to the enclosed back porch that now served as her laundry room. During the renovation, she'd had washer and dryer connections installed, along with a walk-in shower. She could throw her clothes in the washer and scrub the scent of death from her skin and hair before ever setting foot in her house.

Pulling off her T-shirt and shimmying out of her jeans and underwear, she tossed everything in the washer, stepped into the shower and stood under the spray, as hot as she could stand it, scrubbing every inch of her skin and scalp until she could smell nothing but the slightly medicinal aroma of her soap and shampoo. She followed up with a subtle floral fragrance that reminded her of the wild roses that grew in profusion over her back fence.

Wrapped in a towel, she fished clean clothes out of the dryer and dressed right there on the back porch. She wiped down the shower and fiddled with a broken window shade until she realized she was putting off going inside the empty house. Out here she could keep her mind occupied. Inside, she had nothing to do but think.

She went back outside and sat down on the steps, once again letting the dreamy scent of the roses wash over her. Melancholy descended, along with a strange restlessness. She didn't want to dwell on Dr. Nance's death or the upcoming autopsy, so she dug deeper, allowing her mother's specter to come creeping over her defenses.

Nikki didn't think about her parents often. She'd long ago accepted the reality that she would probably never see either of them again. They could both be dead, for all she knew. But sometimes in her weaker moments, she would close her eyes and conjure the two of them together.

Her father had left first, sneaking away in the middle of the night and taking the old Buick and his last paycheck with him. Bitter and broke, Nikki's mother, Joy, had had no choice but to go crawling back home to *her* mother. She'd taken her old bedroom at the back of the house, relegating her ten-year-old daughter to the lumpy couch in the family room. It wouldn't have been so bad for Nikki if her grandfather had still been alive to temper her grandmother's sharp tongue and her mother's resentment. As it was, she found herself hiding out most of the time. Eventually, the three generations had fallen into an uneasy routine until Nikki had come home from school one day to find her mother throwing clothes into a battered suitcase. Nikki remembered that final conversation—every word, every nuance—as if it were yesterday.

Why are you packing, Mama? Are we moving out?

I wish, but where do you think we'd go? Your daddy took the car and every last cent we had when he left. I've managed to save a few bucks from my tips at the diner, so I'm going away with a friend for a little while. I need to get my head on straight and I can't do that here.

Can I come with you?

Not this time. Grandma's old and lonely. She needs you.

She doesn't need me. She doesn't even like me. And she sure as hell doesn't want me here.

You watch your mouth around her, you hear me? Just stay out of her way and everything will be fine.

But why can't I come with you?

Because you can't! I don't expect you to understand any of this right now, but I hope someday you'll look back and realize I'm doing what I think is best for both of us. Your daddy leaving the way he did made me realize that I have to get out, too, else I'll be stuck in this godforsaken town for the rest of my life. I'm young. Still pretty, some say. I'm sorry, Nikki, but I need more out of life than being your mama.

All these years later and Nikki still had a hard time

dealing with what had come next. The pleading and sobbing. The way she'd run down the driveway behind the departing car. She'd been too old to make such a spectacle of herself, or so her grandmother had told her. As painful as it was to remember that day, Nikki had learned a valuable lesson. She would never again give anyone that kind of power over her.

The memory flitted away as her attention snapped back to the present. A sound, a movement... Something had startled her from the past.

For a fleeting moment, Nikki had the uncanny sensation that someone watched her from the shadows. Her mind flashed back to the Ruins and to the way Adam Thayer had stared at her so intently. As if he knew her. Knew things about her. No way he could, of course. There was a reason she kept to herself.

Then she thought about the person they'd spotted on the bank. The way he'd hunkered in the shadows, watching the water, until Adam had turned on his flashlight. Something strange really was going on in Belle Pointe. Nikki just couldn't figure out how she and her missing journal fit into the puzzle.

Rubbing her bare arms, she scoured the landscape. No one was there. Not the man from the lake. Certainly not Adam Thayer. Yet she couldn't shake the feeling of invisible eyes upon her.

It's just those old memories.

She rose and went quickly down the steps into the garden. Her backyard was small. Even with the encroaching darkness, she would be able to spot anyone lurking in the shadows or behind a bush. Nothing was amiss. No intruders. No Peeping Toms.

Circling the garden, she peered behind trees and trellises until satisfied that she was alone. She started to return to the house when she noticed the rear gate ajar. Her property backed up to a wooded area with a footpath on the other side of the creek for joggers and walkers. Nikki was in the habit of keeping the gate bolted so that no one would be tempted to take a shortcut through her yard to the street. She wasn't so much worried for her safety as she valued her privacy.

Someone must have climbed over the fence, unfastened the bolt and then stepped back through to the path without properly closing the gate. Why anyone would do such a thing, she had no idea. Maybe a kid had kicked a ball into her yard or someone had come over the fence chasing a cat. Or maybe the sensation of being watched wasn't so misplaced after all. Maybe someone had been standing just behind the gate, peering through the crack, while she showered and dressed on the back porch.

Revulsion rose like bile in her throat even as she told herself she was letting her imagination get the better of her. She was stressed and not thinking straight. Who wouldn't be? Her friend and mentor lay on a stone-cold slab in the morgue, cause of death still pending. It was certainly possible, perhaps even likely, that he'd suffered a medical event that had precipitated the overturned boat and his spill into the lake. But that didn't explain his sudden change of plans. That didn't explain the hidden watch or the person lurking at the lake the night before. What if he had met with foul play? What if the killer, for whatever reason, now had Nikki in his sights?

You're being ridiculous.

But her pulse wouldn't settle even after she latched the gate and retreated to the safety of her back porch. She made sure the screen and wooden doors were both locked and the windows were all closed before she finally went inside the house.

Everything appeared just as she'd left it that morning and yet nothing was really the same. She went through the motions of checking the refrigerator for dinner, finally settling on a turkey sandwich, but the doorbell interrupted her preparations. Drying her hands, she hurried into the foyer to glance out the sidelight. She rarely had visitors. Except for the occasional dinner with an acquaintance or work colleague, she spent her evenings alone in the garden with a book and her phone.

Lila Wilkes stood on the front porch, clutching a glass pie plate in both hands. Nikki quickly stepped back from the window. Maybe if she pretended she wasn't home, her caller would go away.

Nikki had nothing against the woman—quite the contrary. Lila Wilkes was considered something of a guardian angel in Belle Pointe, always the first to offer a comforting smile and a helping hand in times of sickness and death. Like Dr. Nance, her reputation and regard had created a larger-than-life persona and yet her physical appearance was completely nondescript. She might have been anybody from anywhere with her short gray bob and khaki capris.

Deciding she'd probably been spotted through the window, Nikki pulled the door open. "Mrs. Wilkes! What are you doing here?"

The woman said warmly, "Oh, do call me Lila. I've been a widow for more than thirty years. I don't even feel like Mrs. Wilkes anymore." Her hair was tucked behind her ears, displaying flower earrings that matched the floral print of her top and the sparkly embellishments on her sandals.

"What brings you by...?" Nikki trailed off awkwardly. Even with permission, she had a hard time addressing the woman by her given name.

"I've been baking all day," Lila explained. "I was just out delivering pies to some of our neighbors and I had one left. A blueberry. I thought of you."

"That's very kind." Nikki accepted the pie as she inwardly sighed. Word had already gotten out about Dr. Nance's death. This was either a condolence call or a fishing expedition—possibly both. "Thank you."

Lila craned her neck to glance around Nikki into the house. "I hope I haven't come at a bad time."

Nikki could hardly think of a worse time, but she stepped back from the door. "Would you like to come in?"

"I can only stay a moment." She brushed past Nikki, stopping short in the tiny foyer before advancing into the living area. "My goodness, just look at this place! You've certainly made a lot of changes since you moved in. It doesn't even look like the same house anymore."

Nikki closed the door. "I've done a bit of updating."

"I should say you have," Lila said in wonder. "Everything looks so clean and modern. I prefer traditional, of course, but you're young and single. You have only yourself to please."

Nikki smiled at the backhanded compliment. "I have iced tea in the refrigerator. Would you like some?"

"That would be lovely. If it's not too much trouble."

"No trouble at all."

"We've had such a hot summer. I always long for fall this time of year." She followed Nikki into the kitchen, navigating seamlessly on her platform flip-flops as she circled the small area, taking in the new countertops and cabinets before moving to the French doors to glance out into the backyard. "I see you've kept up the garden. Poor Grace. She worked tirelessly in those beds even after she got sick. She was always so proud of her roses. Second only to mine, everyone said. We dearly miss her in the garden club."

"The bush with the lavender blooms is amazing." Nikki got down two glasses and poured the tea. "I'd never seen roses that color until I bought this house."

"Twilight Mist." Lila smiled dreamily. "Such a romantic name. I gave Grace that cutting years ago. You should see the original bush. The roses are stunning this year. I admire them every morning as I have my coffee." She came over to the counter and sat down on one of the stools, giving a nod of approval after testing her tea. "So refreshing. Not many people can make a truly exceptional pitcher of sweet tea these days. Don't get me started on cold brew and artificial sweeteners."

Nikki left her own glass untouched. "Mrs. Wilkes… Lila…as much as I appreciate your dropping by like this, something tells me you didn't come here to deliver a pie."

"No, dear. I was with Sylvia Navarro early this morning when Billy called about Charles Nance. We were both shocked by the news. Utterly devastated. I know how close the two of you were. He spoke of you as if you were his own granddaughter. I hated thinking of you here all alone. I used the pie as an excuse to come by and see how you're holding up."

Nikki's throat tightened perilously. "I'm okay."

The older woman nodded sympathetically. "I understand Betsy Thayer's grandson found the body. I saw him in town the other day. He's…quite something, isn't he? Such intense eyes. Not very talkative, but you know what they say. Still waters run deep."

Yes, that was an apt description, Nikki thought.

"That young man has lived a life," Lila said. "But that's neither here nor there, is it? Poor Charles. Do you have any idea what happened? Billy said something about a capsized fishing boat."

"An autopsy is pending. I really can't discuss the details until the next of kin have been notified."

Lila paused thoughtfully. "I suppose that would be his nephew, Jeremy. He lives in Atlanta, the last I heard. A few cousins are scattered about, but I don't think Charles was close to any of them. If you ask me, Dessie Dupre is his real family. She worked for the man for the better part of thirty years. Cooked his meals, cleaned his house, tended his garden. She was quite proprietary of his time, too. No one was allowed to drop by that house without calling first." Lila fingered the buttons on her blouse as she stared with a pensive frown into her tea. "If she's not family, I don't know who is."

"I'm sure the sheriff has already spoken to her,"

Nikki murmured, not offering any details about her conversation with Tom Brannon that morning.

"I'm sure he has, too, but maybe you should go see her yourself. Her sister caters our garden club luncheons and sometimes Dessie gives her a hand. We chat during the cleanup. She always speaks so highly of you and all that you've accomplished. I know you'd be a comfort to her at a time like this."

"I'll stop by as soon as I can," Nikki said.

Lila nodded, her voice turning brisk as she mentally took charge. "I wonder if anyone has thought to call Dr. Wingate. I don't know how close she and Charles were personally, but they were business partners for a long time. She'll need to make arrangements for his patients. Then there's the funeral. Flowers, music, eulogy. A hundred and one details to be considered, especially a service befitting someone of Charles Nance's standing."

Nikki could almost hear the gears grinding inside the woman's head. She was in her element now. Nothing suited Lila Wilkes more than planning, organizing and delegating.

"I don't want to think about the funeral tonight," Nikki said. "As far as the interested parties go, Sheriff Brannon's office will make the proper notifications. That's how it works in this county."

"Interested parties. That sounds so impersonal, doesn't it? And yet there is nothing more personal than death." Lila sighed. "But of course, you're right. There'll be plenty of time to make the necessary arrangements in the coming days. We all need time to process and mourn. So many people will be impacted by this death. Charles Nance was the heart of Belle Pointe."

"Some people would argue that you're the heart of this town," Nikki said.

"Me?" She looked pleased. "I do what I can, but no. Charles was our heart and soul. Just look at all the lives he touched. Did you know he's the reason I came to Belle Pointe?"

"I didn't know." Nikki resisted the urge to glance at the time on her phone. "Perhaps you can tell me about it someday."

Lila blithely ignored her cue. "I was living down in Baton Rouge at the time. Only in my twenties, but already a widow. My mother had died a few years earlier and my father had passed when I was small. I was alone in the world, desperate and destitute, not knowing where my next meal would come from, much less how to pay my rent."

"I've been there," Nikki murmured. Except for the widowed part.

"And just look where you are now." Lila beamed. "My salvation came by way of a letter. I've always said my trip to the mailbox that day was divine intervention."

Nikki found her interest piqued despite her impatience. "The letter was from Dr. Nance?"

"It was. I didn't know him at the time, only that he was my aunt Mary's physician. She'd taken ill and had asked him to write to me on her behalf. The letter caught me by surprise. Mary was my mother's sister, but I'd only ever met her once that I could remember. She and my mother had had a falling-out years earlier."

"That's a shame."

"Yes. My mother didn't like to talk about it, so I never knew the details. Anyway, my aunt needed someone to look after her, and seeing as how I was her only living relative, she wondered if I would be willing to come to Belle Pointe and move in with her. My circumstances being what they were, the invitation seemed too good to be true. But after Charles and I spoke on the phone, I accepted her offer. He could be quite convincing when he wanted to be. Charming, too. And, oh, so dashing back in those days." She looked momentarily flustered and laughed at herself. "I'm afraid I had a bit of a crush on him. Everyone did. He was the most handsome and charismatic man I ever knew."

"I never thought of him as a heartthrob," Nikki said.

"Oh, my dear child, you've no idea. Audrey was a very lucky lady. But to make a long story short, a week after we spoke on the phone, I arrived by bus with little more than the clothes on my back."

"It must have been stressful moving in with someone you didn't know," Nikki said.

"*Stressful* is hardly the word. Even though Charles had warned me about my aunt's illness, I was shocked by her condition. A stroke had left her bedridden. She could barely speak or even feed herself without assistance. The responsibility of caring for her seemed overwhelming at first. I often thought about slipping away in the middle of the night, but she needed me. I was all she had, and after a time, I came to love her as if she were my own mother. When she died, I was no longer destitute thanks to her generosity, but once again desperately alone. Then a few weeks later, Mrs. Jensen fell and broke her hip. And Mrs. Witherspoon came down with pneumonia. The point is, there was always someone who needed me. I came to Belle Pointe for my aunt, but the whole town became my family." She reached across the counter and placed her hand on Nikki's. "We can be your family, too, if you'll let us."

Nikki appreciated the gesture. She did. But allowing someone into her life and into her heart wasn't so easy. Everyone she'd ever cared about had left her. She murmured her appreciation as she slipped her hand away. "Thank you. You've been very kind."

"It's the least I can do. I was always sorry I couldn't do more for your poor grandmother." Lila rose. "I'll be on my way now. I've taken up too much of your time as it is. Thank you for indulging a chatty old woman. You call me if you need anything. I mean that sincerely."

"I will." Nikki ushered her out the door.

"And please let me know about the autopsy." She looked suddenly aghast as she stood on the porch steps gazing up at Nikki. "Goodness, that sounded macabre. I just think it would give us all some closure if we knew for certain what happened out there on that lake."

Nikki nodded without comment. She stood on the porch and watched Lila Wilkes's taillights disappear around the corner. As the sound of the car engine faded, the neighborhood fell quiet. Clouds covered the moon so that only the streetlamps kept the gloom at bay. With the gathering darkness, apprehension once again descended.

Nikki scanned the nightscape, unable to shake the notion that someone was out there in the shadows watching her house, watching *her*, but why?

Chapter Five

Adam cut the engine and drifted through the tangle of water lilies toward the bank. This was the first time he'd taken his grandmother's twelve-foot johnboat out on the water since hauling it down from storage. After making sure the aluminum hull was still sound, he'd purchased a small outboard motor for tooling around the lake. The horsepower wouldn't win any races, but he didn't plan on needing much speed. At the moment, he was much more concerned about stealth.

All day long, he'd worked outside so that he could keep an eye on Dr. Nance's cabin. Two of Tom Brannon's officers had come out early that morning to search the property and the surrounding woods. After they left, Adam had been sorely tempted to take the boat across the lake right then and there, but he'd told himself to wait for darkness. The last thing he needed was to be caught in broad daylight breaking and entering a dead man's house.

Although, technically, he didn't need to break in. Dr. Nance had told him where he could find a spare key in case his grandmother's house was unlivable. Still, it was best to avoid getting jammed up with local law enforcement, so Adam had watched the water and waited.

Sure enough, a little while ago, Tom Brannon and his officers had come back out to the cabin to take another look around. Adam had lingered on the dock, tracking their movements by the bobble of their flashlights. One of them had come down to the bank and shone his light across the water, catching Adam in the beam. Adam had lifted his hand in a brief salute and stubbornly stayed put while the light washed over the dock and climbed the stairs behind him.

After the cops drove off, Adam had climbed down into the fishing boat and started the outboard. Seated at the tiller, he'd navigated across the dark water using the faint shimmer of moonlight from behind thin clouds to guide him.

Now he let the prow run aground beneath a thick curtain of Spanish moss, then hopped out of the boat and grabbed his flashlight. He had no idea what he might find in the cabin. He didn't even know what he was looking for. The notes and files that Dr. Nance had mentioned during their last phone call? The sheriff and his officers would have bagged and documented any evidence they'd come across, but Adam knew he wouldn't rest until he'd been through the cabin himself.

He climbed the steep steps, glancing over his shoulder now and then to scour the water and the surrounding woods. He could see the silhouette of his grandmother's house across the lake and, farther down the bank, the twinkling lights on Ellie Brannon's antenna. This time of night, she would probably be in her tiny studio, getting ready for her radio broadcast. Adam had listened to her show once or twice since he moved in. *Midnight on Echo Lake*, she called it. Strange show. Strange callers. Not his thing. He had no interest in the supernatural, but he had to admit if any place could be haunted, it would be Echo Lake. If souls could be trapped, they would surely linger inside the Ruins.

The bullfrogs on this side of the lake had gone silent upon his arrival. The woods seemed darker than usual and eerily quiet. Adam missed the noises of the city. Squealing tires, blaring horns. An endless cacophony of sirens. On the day of the shooting, the same uncanny hush had settled over the residential street where he and his partner had gone to serve a warrant. No kids on the sidewalk. No garbage trucks, no yard crews. Adam remembered standing at the top of the porch steps and looking out over the street as he took in that strange silence. A split second later, all hell had broken loose.

He shook himself out of the past, running a hand over the top of his head as his gaze traveled across the lake and along the bank. Nothing moved. Nothing so much as a stray breeze stirred, and yet he couldn't shake a vague premonition that something was wrong.

He searched the darkness for a moment longer before he climbed up to the deck. Locating the key beneath the seat cushion of an old blue rocking chair, he let himself in through the French doors and paused once more to gather his bearings. Then he turned on the flashlight and moved the beam slowly around the space.

The cabin was small, with the kitchen to his left, the living area straight ahead and the bedroom and bathroom to his right. He crossed the room and glanced out the front window. Dr. Nance's Jeep was parked in the gravel driveway. Adam went out the door and down the porch steps to check the vehicle. The doors were locked. He shone the light inside and then walked slowly around the vehicle, checking for body damage or bloodstains.

Finding nothing suspicious, he switched off the light and stood listening to the night. He could hear the distant putter of an outboard motor somewhere on the lake, but the boat seemed to be moving away from the cabin. He waited for another moment before heading back inside to search each room.

A closed suitcase rested on the bed, but smaller personal items like Dr. Nance's wallet, phone and keys were nowhere to be found. Either they'd been confiscated as evidence or they had fallen into the water when the boat capsized. Or someone besides the police had taken them. Adam made fast work of the tidy closet and chest of drawers, and then returned to the main area of the cabin.

A well-worn recliner was positioned near the fireplace so that in the winter Dr. Nance could enjoy a crackling blaze while admiring the sunset. The side table was piled high with books and magazines. A small desk occupied the opposite side of the room. Adam quickly went through the drawers and then searched the kitchen cupboards. He even checked the refrigerator and freezer before returning to Dr. Nance's recliner. After glancing at the address label on one of the magazines, he thumbed through the pages and then scanned the book titles. The reading material varied, everything from fishing magazines to crime thrillers to World War II nonfiction. Even among that eclectic collection, one of the titles leaped out at him: *The Ingenious Gentleman Don Quixote of La Mancha.*

There was nothing strange about a man who enjoyed classic literature. Dr. Nance appeared to have been a voracious and curious reader. But that particular title stopped Adam cold as his mind raced back to their last conversation. *If you get here and decide I'm just a delusional old coot tilting at windmills...*

Maybe he was reaching, Adam thought. Maybe he was the one tilting at windmills, but he'd never been a big believer in coincidences. Had Dr. Nance used that particular phrase for a reason? Had he deliberately left the book in plain sight at the cabin?

Adam sat down in the recliner and flipped through the pages, then carefully examined the binding. It took several minutes of searching before he found the tiny rolled piece of paper that had been slipped up into the spine of the book where the stitching had come loose. He used a pen to carefully fish it out. The note contained a handwritten number in blue ink: 47.

He flipped to page forty-seven and read the text. If there was a clue hidden within the dialogue about knight-errantry, it was lost on Adam.

Reaching for his phone, he snapped a shot of the note, then rerolled the paper and returned it to the spine of the book. He took another quick survey of the cabin before he doused the flashlight and went out the same way he'd come in. He was still at the top of the steps when he spotted a boat gliding across the lake without lights or an engine.

Clouds smothered all but a faint shimmer of moonlight. The night was very dark and yet there was no mistaking the movement of the boat or the distant splash of water against oars. He could just make out the silhouette of the rower as he bent to his task. For a moment, Adam thought the small craft might drift right up to the spot where he'd left his grandmother's boat, but instead the prow turned toward the dock, making it impossible for Adam to descend the steps without being seen.

Retreating back into the cabin, he purposefully left the latches unlocked and then hid behind the bedroom door, positioning himself so that he could peer out into the other room. A few minutes went by before a figure wearing a black hoodie appeared on the deck.

A face pressed against the glass, but Adam couldn't make out his features. The man looked to be taller than average with a muscular build. He lifted his hand and shone a flashlight beam into the space before trying the latches. Adam sank back from the opening. The light went out, and a moment later, he heard the hinges squeak as the doors opened, and then footsteps thudded across the wooden floor.

The intruder's movements were efficient but unhurried as he made his way around the cabin, searching through the desk and side table drawers, then turning his attention to the bathroom and finally the bedroom. Adam had never shied away from confrontation, but at the moment, he was far more interested in finding out what the intruder might be after. He dropped to the floor and rolled silently under the bed.

The man entered the room and moved around the space, opening drawers and the closet door and then pausing beside the bed while Adam held his breath. The intruder lingered as though sensing a presence. Adam braced for an attack. Already the adrenaline was starting to pump. But the man turned and went back into the main room. The footsteps receded, the French doors clicked shut and he was gone.

Adam slid from underneath the bed and glanced into the other room, scouting all the shadowy corners before locking the doors and easing across the deck. He paused once again to scan the area, but the man in black had vanished.

Keeping to the shadows, Adam slipped down the steps far enough to see the dock. The boat was still tied off. The intruder hadn't gone far.

Whether Adam heard a slight noise, he saw something out of the corner of his eye, or his instincts were that highly attuned to the night, he didn't know, but he immediately ducked. A bullet whizzed past his cheek, exploding the bark of a pine tree to his right as the crack of gunfire echoed out over the water.

For one stunned moment, Adam was back in Dallas, back on that porch with the sound of gunfire ringing in his ears. He hadn't worn body armor that day. It was supposed to be a routine arrest. Nothing to worry about. Nothing at all out of the ordinary. Just as this should have been a routine search of Dr. Nance's cabin. No one else was supposed to be here.

For what seemed an eternity, Adam hunkered on the steps, partially concealed by the overgrown vegetation and the encroaching shadows. He told himself to move, take cover, and yet he remained captive to a deadly paralysis. He could see the shooter out of the corner of his eye. The man hovered at the top of the stairs as if waiting to see if he'd hit his mark. He came down the steps slowly at first and then in a rush, surprisingly fleet of foot for someone his size.

Adam reacted on instinct just as he had after the Dallas shooting. That day, he'd bled profusely from his wounds as he crawled to the corner of the house seeking cover. He didn't remember anything else. He'd never even heard the sirens.

Tonight, there were no sirens. No sound at all once the echo of gunfire had died away over the water. The humid night seemed to close in on him as he crouched in the bushes and waited. He drew a breath and then another, settling his nerves before maneuvering into a position where he could glimpse the stairs. The footsteps had gone silent. He could imagine the shooter pausing to listen for a snapping twig or a hitched breath. Anything that would give away his quarry's position.

The cloudy sky worked in Adam's favor now. He couldn't see the shooter from his vantage, but neither could the shooter see him. Questions lurked at the back of his mind. Who was this guy and what had he been looking for in Dr. Nance's cabin? Adam pushed the queries aside and concentrated on what he did know. He was unarmed, so surprise was his best weapon.

A wooden step creaked and then another as the shooter descended cautiously. The notion crossed Adam's mind that he should try to make a quiet getaway. He was outsized and unarmed; just slip away into the night. But another creak and he was on his feet, endorphins surging. He lunged, tackling the man around the knees, and he heard the satisfying thud of the gun hitting a wooden step as they crashed to the ground. The shooter's fingers closed around Adam's throat as Adam's thumbs dug into the man's eyes. Neither gave ground. On and on they fought as they tumbled down the steps toward the dock.

Adam's head cracked against one of the metal cleats bolted into the wood. Blood and white-hot pain temporarily blinded him. Dazed, he wiped his eyes as he staggered to his feet. His opponent was hardly more than a hulking shadow in the dark. He lowered his head like a bull and slammed into Adam. The impact knocked the breath from his lungs and toppled him backward into the lake.

Surfacing, he caught his breath on a gasp, almost expecting his opponent to jump into the water to try to finish him off. A million thoughts rushed through his head as the adrenaline continued to pump. He shook water from his eyes and ears and searched the darkness. Footsteps pounded up the steps. The assailant had gone back for his gun.

Adam tried to hitch himself up on the dock, but a volley of shots forced him back into the lake. The man came running down the steps, peppering the water with bullets. Adam pushed away from the dock and dived, swimming out into deeper water for cover. He stayed under until his lungs screamed for air, and when he surfaced, he heard the putter of a small outboard, which had been silent earlier. He treaded water until a spotlight caught him in the eyes. The boat was almost upon him before he once again dived for the murky bottom and swam out toward the middle of the lake.

The night was pitch-black above and beneath the

surface. Disoriented, Adam hung suspended as he tried to get his bearings. Once upon a time, he'd been able to hold his breath for a very long time, but that was before he'd taken two bullets in the chest. He surfaced a third time, gasping for air as he searched for the boat. His head throbbed; his lungs burned. For weeks, he'd been intensifying his workouts, fooling himself into thinking he was fully recovered. His muscles now told him otherwise. He was already fatigued.

The outboard rumbled off into the distance. He waited until the sound had disappeared into the night and then he rolled over on his back and floated. He couldn't stay out on the lake forever. Already the adrenaline was giving way to a dangerous lethargy. Setting out toward the bank, he measured his strokes and controlled his breathing until he could stand up in knee-deep water. Exhausted, he sloshed back toward the dock. He'd lost his phone somewhere along the way. He imagined it at the bottom of the lake, along with the photograph of Dr. Nance's mysterious note.

He still had no idea of the significance of that number. He couldn't begin to guess what Dr. Nance may have stumbled upon.

What he did know was that someone had been willing to put a bullet in him tonight.

Chapter Six

A storm blew in after midnight, and a loud clap of thunder awakened Nikki with a start. She fluffed her pillow and pulled the covers up to her chin, but she couldn't fall back asleep.

Rolling to her back, she watched shadows dance across the ceiling, hoping the hypnotic motion would lull her back under. She only grew more and more anxious. Finally, she kicked off the quilt and rose to wander restlessly through the house. After pouring herself a glass of water, she went out to the back porch, where she could watch the storm through the screen door.

The wind chimes clanked in the gusts and the rain deepened the scent of roses and wet grass. In the flare of a lightning strike, Nikki could have sworn she saw a tall man dressed in dark clothing standing just inside the back gate.

She straightened with a gasp, her heart flailing against her rib cage as she peered through the darkness. For a split second only, she thought about going out to investigate, but a voice that sounded suspiciously like her grandmother's froze her in place. *Girl, are you stupid or just plain crazy? Don't go out there alone.*

He could be an ax murderer, for all you know. Go in-side and call the police.

But the figure she'd spotted in one lightning strike vanished in the next, leaving Nikki to wonder if she'd seen nothing more than a small tree that grew along the fence. She stood behind the latched screen door and scanned the yard until her pulse finally settled and she managed to convince herself the lightning and her imagination had conjured the intruder. No one had been in her yard earlier. No one was out there now. *Go back to bed.*

She closed the wooden door and turned the dead bolt, then checked all the windows on the porch before padding back off to bed. Climbing under the covers, she lay wide-awake as the flickers of lightning gradually grew dimmer and thunder faded in the distance. She was just growing drowsy when she heard a car start up down the street.

Nasty night to be out so late, she thought. The vehicle seemed to slow as it approached her house.

She got up and glanced out the window. A truck lumbered by, splashing water to the curb. The back was enclosed like a delivery vehicle of some sort, but who would be getting a package at this hour?

Nikki told herself the driver was just being cautious in the storm. He hadn't intentionally slowed for her house. She really was letting her imagination get the better of her. No one had been in the backyard watching her house. No one had waited behind the garden gate for her lights to go out. She'd summoned the boogeymen of her childhood so she wouldn't have to succumb to her grief. But it was coming. Sooner or later, she would have to deal with another loss.

She snuggled deeper under the covers and closed her eyes on a shiver.

When she awakened again it was to sunshine streaming across her face. Birds chirped in the tree outside her bedroom window and she could hear the normal, everyday sound of traffic on the street. Relieved to have another bad night behind her, she crawled out of bed, showered and dressed in her usual uniform of jeans, sneakers and T-shirt. Then she headed to the lab, where she changed into scrubs, lab coat, goggles and mask.

Dr. Ramirez came in a few minutes later, and they began the autopsy on Dr. Nance's remains. Nikki tried to distance herself from the process as she assisted in examining, removing and weighing the internal organs and in collecting blood and tissue samples. The procedure took little more than two hours. Only when the Y-shaped incision had been stitched did she step out into the hallway for a moment to catch her breath and steady her emotions.

As she feared, the preliminary findings were inconclusive. She delivered the results later that day to Sheriff Brannon in person.

He motioned her to a chair across from his desk while he took a moment to scan the report. "Says here the findings are consistent with drowning."

Nikki nodded. "We found froth in the mouth, nostrils and trachea, and that, along with the elevated lung weight and pleural effusions, would suggest death by drowning. We're waiting for some of the other test results before we reach a consensus. The toxicology screen could take a couple of weeks. Once everything is in, Dr. Ramirez will provide a more detailed analysis in his final report."

Tom got up and closed his office door. "You're satisfied with these findings?"

"If you mean as coroner, am I ready to rule the death an accidental drowning? No, not yet. I still want to know why and how he ended up at the lake when he was supposed to be at a conference in Houston. Something doesn't feel right to me, Tom. Despite that, I find it hard to believe anyone would want to harm Dr. Nance. What would be the motive?"

"Motive will sometimes surprise you." Tom sat back down and picked up the report. "I haven't been able to track down the conference coordinator to confirm a cancellation, but we did find Dr. Nance's Jeep at the cabin. The house was locked up. Dessie Dupre gave us a key to get in. No sign of a forced entry or struggle inside. We found his closed suitcase on the bed and his wallet, car fob and phone on the nightstand. There was cash in the wallet, along with his driver's license, credit cards and insurance information. He cleaned out his pockets but didn't take time to unpack before going out in the boat."

"But why?" Nikki fell silent as she pondered the possibilities. Something occurred to her. "Did you find his journal at the cabin?"

Tom glanced up. "He kept a journal?"

"For as long as I've known him. He's the one who persuaded me to journal when I was younger. I kept one faithfully for years, but it got to be too much work."

And too dangerous. Nikki paused, thinking about her secret hiding place at the Ruins and wondering again who may have stumbled upon her confession. "Anyway, if we can find his notes, maybe some of our questions will be answered."

"I'll run by his house later and see if Dessie knows anything about it. She may have remembered something else, too, since we last talked. What about his medical history? Anything there?"

"We had his records sent over before the autopsy. He had a physical last year. Other than mild hypertension, he was in good health for a man his age."

"So that brings us back to his mental state."

Nikki winced. She hated thinking about Dr. Nance out on the lake, perhaps lost and confused. Or in a moment of clarity, contemplating what might lie ahead of him. She tried to shake off a creeping despair. "As I said before, he seemed fine when I saw him last week."

Tom glanced up. "You also said you were in a hurry to get back to work and may have missed something."

"Your point?"

He leaned back in his chair. "I spoke to Dr. Wingate this morning. She told me there'd been some problems at the clinic lately."

Nikki frowned. "What kind of problems?"

"Memory issues. Forgotten appointments, duplicated tests. He even mixed up two prescriptions. The mistake was caught in time, but when Dr. Wingate brought the error to his attention, he couldn't remember writing either prescription. After that incident, she said he began referring most of his patients to her. He planned to phase out his practice altogether when he returned from the conference in Houston."

"That's strange," Nikki said. "He never said anything to me about retiring."

"Maybe he didn't want to worry you. Or maybe he just needed time to process the idea before he made an announcement."

"Why go to a medical conference if he planned to retire?"

"To see old friends, maybe. Who knows? Maybe that's why he changed his mind and went to the lake instead." Tom paused thoughtfully. "How well do you know Dr. Wingate?"

"I've met her a few times. She's what my grandmother would have called a cold fish. Not exactly a desirable bedside manner in a family physician. Why do you ask?"

"I picked up a vibe when we talked. She seemed guarded and evasive. Did she and Dr. Nance ever have any trouble?"

"Not that I know of. What are you getting at?"

He swiveled his chair toward the window and glanced out at the street, taking a long moment to answer. "I just want to make sure we don't overlook anything. Once a death is ruled an accident, it's hard to go back from that. Evidence gets lost or contaminated. Witnesses forget what they saw. I don't want to make any mistakes."

Nikki stared at him for a moment. "Tom. Are you telling me you think his death *wasn't* an accident?"

"No—the opposite, in fact. The most likely scenario is accidental drowning, but that's why I'm being cautious. I don't want to get tunnel vision or jump to any conclusions before we have all the facts. But I also can't ignore what people are telling me."

"People other than Dr. Wingate?"

He rubbed the back of his neck. "Dessie told me she'd also had some concerns about Dr. Nance's recent behavior. She said he almost always had a drink out on the porch before dinner. Or sometimes he'd take a dip in the pool. Lately, though, he'd go straight to his study and close the door as soon as he came home from the clinic. Sometimes Dessie would have to knock several times to get his attention. When she asked what he was working on, he told her he was trying to put together a puzzle."

"A puzzle? What did he mean by that?"

Tom shrugged. "Your guess is as good as mine. Like I said, I'll go over and talk to Dessie again later, see if she knows anything about the journal. Maybe she can help clear up a few other questions, too. She was pretty upset when we talked yesterday."

"We're all upset." Nikki had been so distraught she'd imagined someone standing in the backyard, watching her house.

"It's got to be especially hard on her," Tom said. "She's not only lost a friend, but also her whole way of life. Not much call for live-in housekeepers in Belle Pointe."

"I'm sure Dr. Nance left provisions in his will. The two of them were always close."

Tom pounced. "How close?"

"What exactly are you asking?"

He picked up a pen and fiddled with the cap. "I think you know what I'm asking."

Nikki gaped at him. "Dessie and Dr. Nance? You can't be serious."

He tossed aside the pen. "They were all alone in that big house, night after night, year after year. Neither of them attached. Human nature is what it is, Nikki."

"She had her own place over the garage. Besides, she was at least twenty years younger than he was."

"So?"

"You're way off base. I was in that house a lot as a kid. Sometimes I'd help Dessie cook and clean for a little spending money. When I was finished, I'd sit out on the porch with Dr. Nance while he told the most hilarious stories about his med school days. Dessie would serve us sweet tea and gingersnaps. Sometimes she'd linger to hear one of his yarns, but I never sensed anything remotely romantic between them." Nikki gave him a dubious look. "Is this still your way of making sure you don't overlook anything? Because it sounds a lot like grasping at straws to me. You can't possibly think Dessie had anything to do with Dr. Nance's death. She was devoted to the man."

Tom answered her question with another question. "What do you make of Adam Thayer?"

"I... What?" He'd caught her by surprise.

Tom didn't seem to notice her stammering hesitation. He plowed on without waiting for a response. "According to Thayer, Dr. Nance called him early last week and asked him to come to Belle Pointe. He said something strange was going on down here. Something dark."

"I know. Adam told me the same thing."

He lifted a brow at her use of the man's first name.

"Like Dr. Wingate, he was worried about Dr. Nance's mental state. Three people voicing concerns about his behavior can't be dismissed out of hand."

Nikki nodded. "It's just so distressing. After everything Dr. Nance did for me, how could I have let this happen? How could I have talked to him last week and not sensed something was wrong? If I'd been more attentive, maybe he'd still be alive."

"Don't take that burden on yourself," Tom advised. "People hide things. Sometimes even from themselves."

She smiled forlornly. Yes. She knew all about keeping things hidden.

It was a strange turn of events, Adam decided. Nikki Dresden had been on his mind all morning as he'd worked around his grandmother's house. She was still on his mind when he'd taken the boat across the lake to search for the embedded bullet in the pine tree and then later when he'd driven into town to replace his phone. Now, as he approached the front entrance of the county sheriff's office, there she was in person. Head slightly bowed, her brow furrowed.

Deep in thought, she walked out the door and bumped right into him. She quickly stepped back, looking unaccountably flustered. In the split second before she moved away, he could have sworn he smelled the scent of roses wafting from her hair.

What struck him more forcefully were her eyes. They were a deep, rich brown. No gold or green flecks, just dark, fathomless pools. He could see a sprinkling of freckles across her nose and a tiny indented scar at her jawline. Not perfect, not beautiful, and yet, like before, he found her enigmatic. Dangerously intriguing.

"I'm sorry," they both said at once.

"No, it was my fault. I wasn't looking where I was going." Her cheeks colored as she self-consciously tucked back her hair. She wore it loose today. The ends turned under at her shoulders, gleaming like a raven's wing in the sun. She got a good look at him then, her gaze taking in the cut above his eyebrow and the bruises on his cheekbone. "What happened to you?"

"Let's just say I ran up against a tank."

"A tank?" Her gaze dropped to his taped knuckles. "That must have been some collision."

He didn't comment. "I'm glad I ran into you this morning. You're just the person I've been wanting to see."

Something flashed in her eyes. Hesitation? Curiosity? "What about?"

"I'd like to talk to you about Dr. Nance, if you have a minute."

She glanced over her shoulder at the station entrance. "Weren't you going inside?"

"Yes, but maybe I could swing by your office afterward."

A frown flitted. "I'm not going into my office today. Why don't you just tell me what this is about?"

"I'd rather not get into it on the street," Adam said. "Can I buy you a cup of coffee? The diner is just a few blocks over. It's an easy walk from here."

Her expression was easy to read. She wanted to turn him down but not as much as she wanted to hear what he had to say about Dr. Nance.

"There's a coffee shop just down the street. That's more convenient. I only have a few minutes," she warned. "There's someplace I need to be."

"Not a problem. This won't take long." His phone rang and he glanced at the screen, noting the name with a scowl. Meredith Cassidy was the police psychologist assigned to his case after the shooting in Dallas. Stress debriefings and trauma intervention following a major event were routine in large police departments, or so Adam had always thought. He wondered how he'd remained so naive all these years. A decade with the Dallas PD and he was just now learning how politically motivated psych evaluations could be.

"Trouble?" Nikki asked.

He realized he was still frowning at his phone and he gave her an apologetic glance. "No, but I should probably take this. I'll make it quick."

She looked as if she regretted agreeing to their talk, but then she shrugged and nodded. "Go ahead. I'll wait for you at the coffee shop. Straight ahead and to the right. You can't miss it."

"Wait!"

She'd already started to walk away, but turned when he called out to her.

"Does the number forty-seven mean anything to you?" he asked.

She looked puzzled. "What?"

"The number forty-seven. Did it have special significance to Dr. Nance?"

"Of course it did."

Her matter-of-fact response startled him. "What does it mean?"

Her gaze dropped to his phone. "Take your call. We can talk about it when you're finished."

He watched her walk away as he lifted the phone to his ear.

"Hello, Dr. Cassidy. Can I assume you're calling to tell me you've signed off on my reinstatement?"

"I only wish it were that simple, Adam. You've missed your last two appointments. You know I can't recommend you for active duty until you come back in and talk things through with me."

"Haven't we already done that?" He squinted into the sun as he eyed the park across the street. A man wearing a baseball cap and sunglasses sat on a shaded bench, texting on his phone. He was a big guy and Adam's mind instantly flashed back to the gunfire last night, to the near miss on the steps and the spray of bullets in the water. He couldn't say with any certainty that the man on the bench was the shooter. He'd never gotten a good look at the suspect. But the stranger's proximity to the police station made Adam wonder if he'd been followed from the lake into town.

As if prodded by Adam's scrutiny, the man glanced up. When he saw that he'd been spotted, he rose from the bench and walked quickly away.

"Adam? Are you there?"

He'd forgotten about the therapist. Adam stepped off the curb, phone still to his ear. "Yes, I'm here."

"Are you still having nightmares?"

"No. As a matter of fact, I'm sleeping like a baby these days."

"And the headaches?"

He hesitated. "Better."

"Well, these seem like significant developments," she said encouragingly. "Why don't you make an appointment for sometime next week? We can discuss any other changes, good or bad, you may be experiencing."

He glanced both ways before crossing the street. A horn blared and he put up a hand as he hurried out of the way of oncoming traffic. The man in the park glanced back at the commotion. The bill of the cap was pulled low over his face, shading his features. He paused for a moment as if daring Adam to pursue him. Then he turned and headed down one of the pathways toward the wooded area of the park.

"Adam? Are you all right? You seem distracted."

He pressed the phone to his ear. "I'm fine. I'm out of town at the moment. I'll have to give you a ring when I get back to Dallas."

"Where are you?"

"We'll talk soon, Doc."

He ended the call and slipped the phone in his pocket as he opened the park gate and stepped through. It was a busy place. Kids were out of school for the summer and looking for a place to hang out. In a quieter corner, mothers and caregivers sat reading or chatting on shady benches while toddlers and preschoolers played nearby.

Adam was acutely aware of all those soft targets. He slowed, putting distance between himself and the man in the ball cap. One thing to risk his own hide, but quite another when it came to innocent bystanders.

Only when his quarry had disappeared into the trees did Adam speed his steps, keeping an eye on his surroundings as the sound of laughter faded in the back-ground.

The trees thickened as the paved pathway gave way to a series of dirt jogging trails. The oak leaf canopy blocked the sun so that it was cool and dim in the woods. Lots of shadows. Lots of places to hide.

He didn't meet a single soul on the trail. He might have been in the middle of nowhere but for the occasional shriek of laughter behind him and the muted sound of traffic in front of him. He came out of the trees onto another busy street. He glanced over his shoulder. Glanced both ways down the sidewalk. The man in the ball cap was nowhere to be found.

Adam waited for a few minutes longer before he turned and retraced the trail through the woods. He came out on the other side of the park, transitioning from the shade into the brilliant glare of sunlight. He walked down to the nearest intersection to cross back over. He had the light. The truck came out of nowhere. Bigger than a pickup. A utility or delivery vehicle of some sort. An old model covered in dark gray primer.

He observed all this in the space of a heartbeat as the truck roared through the intersection. The driver swerved, and Adam stepped back up on the sidewalk, certain the maniac intended to jump the curb and come straight at him. At the last minute, the vehicle careened back into traffic and barreled down the street, barely slowing to make the next corner.

Gazing after the truck, Adam committed to memory what he remembered of the vehicle. There hadn't been a license plate, he realized.

He waited for another light and crossed the street, keeping an eye on oncoming traffic.

Two near misses in less than twenty-four hours. Not a coincidence. Not by a long shot. Someone was coming for him.

Chapter Seven

Nikki looked up expectantly as Adam entered the coffee shop. She'd begun to think he wasn't going to show. Not that it mattered to her one way or the other, she told herself. She was happy enough to just get on with the rest of her day. But there he was.

He stood inside the doorway, searching for her among the handful of patrons, and then his gaze lingered before he turned to the barista and placed an order.

From a distance he looked fine. Nikki could hardly see the bruises. He might not be the golden boy from her memory, but the older, tougher, more jaded man wasn't without cachet. She acknowledged his appeal even as she cautioned herself to maintain a neutral perspective. She barely knew Adam Thayer, and the little she'd learned of him was hardly reassuring. She prided herself on keeping an open mind, but never at the expense of common sense.

Coffee in hand, he gave her a brief nod as he wound his way through the maze of tables and chairs.

She returned his greeting with a slight smile. "I was beginning to think you weren't coming."

"I'm sorry. That took a lot longer than I expected." He sat down across from her. "Thanks for waiting."

"Of course." Her gaze swept over his face. "Are you sure you're okay? That cut above your eyebrow looks pretty deep."

"I cleaned it up with antiseptic. It should be fine."

"Watch out for infection," she advised. "Are you going to tell me how you really got all those cuts and bruises?"

"Yes, but that explanation will have to wait. I know you don't have a lot of time, so I want to get this out of the way first. What can you tell me about Dr. Nance's autopsy?"

Nikki's guard went up. "How do you know he's even been autopsied yet?"

"Given his standing in the community and the questions surrounding his death, I'm assuming he'd be a priority. Plus, I drove by the forensic science center earlier. I saw your vehicle in the staff parking lot."

"That's a thirty-minute drive one way," she said.

"I had some time to kill." He lifted his cup, observing her over the top. "The autopsy?"

Such intense eyes. Lila Wilkes had been right about his gaze. "I know you think you have a vested interest in this case, but you're not the only one who feels that way," Nikki said. "A lot of people in this town owe their lives to Dr. Nance. They'd all like to know what happened to him. I'll tell you what I would tell any one of them. If you're not a close relative, then you need to direct your queries to Sheriff Brannon."

He wasn't fazed. "Autopsy reports are a matter of public record. You and I both know I can get my hands on a copy, but that'll take time and I'll have to jump through a lot of annoying hoops. You could save me the trouble by just telling me what you found. Or didn't find."

She hesitated, then relented with a shrug. "It'll probably end up in the paper or online anyway. The preliminary results are consistent with drowning. That's all I'm prepared to say at this time."

He sat back in his chair without comment.

Nikki gazed across the table at him. "You were expecting something else?"

"Not necessarily. I assume you're still waiting on the toxicology screen?"

"That could take days or even weeks. Unless there's reason to suspect foul play, the lab won't prioritize."

"Can you show me the preliminary autopsy report?"

"No, sorry. I'm afraid you'll have to jump through those hoops for that."

He nodded. "Fair enough. I appreciate your candor."

Nikki hesitated. "Can I ask you a question?"

"Shoot."

She folded her arms on the table, relaxing into the conversation. "Why is this so important to you? You say you came to town at Dr. Nance's request, but you can't have known him that long."

"Long enough to consider him a friend." He glanced out the window, squinting into the sun. "I told him I would come down here and have a look around, and that's just what I intend to do. I don't go back on my word because the circumstances have changed. If anything, his death makes me more determined."

"Even if there's nothing to find?"

"I'm not convinced of that yet."

Nikki felt a warning prickle at the base of her spine. "You don't think his death was an accident, do you? Why?"

"Aside from what he told me on the phone? I have my reasons."

Nikki glanced around, lowering her voice to a near whisper. A few other patrons were scattered around the small shop. She wanted to make sure they couldn't overhear the conversation. The last thing Belle Pointe needed was another wave of rumors. "You said he didn't sound himself when he called. He was paranoid and distracted. Those were your words. You said you were worried about his mental state."

"That's right." He leaned in, locking gazes. "I might still have thought he was a little off his rocker if someone hadn't shot at me last night as I was leaving his cabin."

Nikki's mouth dropped open. *"What?"* She took another quick glance around the shop. "Did you see who it was? Tell me what happened."

"I never got a good look. It was too dark and he had a hoodie pulled over his face."

Nikki's mind flashed back to the silhouette she'd glimpsed in her backyard during the storm. She'd managed to convince herself she'd seen nothing more than a tree. The lightning had played tricks on her vision. No one had been watching her house. But now—

"What's wrong?" Adam asked. "You look like you just saw a ghost."

She glanced up. "Not a ghost. I thought I saw someone in my backyard last night. He may or may not have been wearing a hoodie."

Adam's voice sharpened. "When was this?"

"During the storm, so it must have been after midnight. The thunder woke me up. I got up for a drink of water and went out to the back porch to watch the weather. The lightning was pretty keen at that point. It lit up the backyard. That's when I saw someone standing just inside my gate."

"What did he look like? Can you describe him?"

"Not really. I only caught a glance. I thought it was just my imagination. I'm still not certain I saw anything other than a tree or a bush."

"The guy at the cabin was big," Adam said. "Tall and muscular but quick on his feet."

Her gaze flicked to his cuts and bruises. "Did he do that to you?"

"Did he kick my ass, you mean? Yeah. Right after he tried to shoot me."

"Through all that, you never saw his face?"

His gaze turned wry. "I was a little busy fighting for my life."

Nikki took a moment to visualize the fight. "Do you think he could be the same person we saw on the lake two nights ago?"

"I wouldn't discount it."

"I wonder what he was doing at Dr. Nance's cabin."

"Maybe the same thing he was doing on the lake— looking for something," Adam said. "Right now we need to figure out who he is and what he wants, because I think the same guy tried to run me down on my way here."

"Just now, you mean?" Nikki's pulse quickened. This was all getting to be too real. Hard to rationalize one incident after another as coincidental. Assuming Adam Thayer was telling the truth, and she had no reason to doubt him. What if someone really had been in her backyard last night? What if Dr. Nance's death hadn't been an accident after all?

But why would someone come after her? Or Adam Thayer, for that matter? What *dark thing* was going on in Belle Pointe?

His gaze deepened as if he'd read her mind. "Are you sure you're okay?"

"Yes, I'm fine. But this is all pretty unnerving," she said. "Someone shot at you and tried to run you down. Could this be related to the incident in Dallas?"

"The incident?"

Her gaze lifted to the scar across his scalp. "The shooting. Could someone have followed you here?"

"I doubt it. Why would someone who tailed me to Belle Pointe end up in your backyard? No, I think this is all somehow tied to Dr. Nance's drowning."

Nikki drew a breath and nodded. "I'm afraid it's beginning to look that way. I don't suppose you can identify the driver?"

He took a sip of the cooling coffee and winced. "It happened too fast, and looking back, I think the windows must have been tinted. Whoever this guy is, he knows how to keep his face concealed. I can describe the vehicle, though. It was an old panel truck covered in primer. There wasn't a plate. For a moment, I thought the driver was going to jump the curb and plow right into me. He swerved back into traffic at the last minute."

"Did anyone else see it happen?"

"There were other cars on the road, but I was the only pedestrian at that intersection. I'll check to see if any of the businesses in the immediate vicinity have security cams. That might be our best bet in tracking him down."

Nikki said slowly, "I saw that truck go by my house last night. Or one very much like it."

He glanced up. "Before or after you spotted someone in your backyard?"

"After. I heard a vehicle start up down the street and I got up to look out the window. I remember thinking how odd it was to see a delivery truck at that time of night, much less in the middle of a storm."

"I have to say, this is getting stranger and stranger," Adam muttered.

Yeah, no kidding.

"You don't remember seeing a vehicle like that around town?" he asked.

"Delivery trucks, sure, but not an old one covered in primer." Nikki paused, her gaze once more roaming over the other customers. Most of them were absorbed in their coffee and phones. No one seemed to take notice of the couple seated by the window engaged in an intense conversation. But she kept her voice down anyway. "What were you doing at Dr. Nance's cabin last night?"

"I took my grandmother's boat over to have a look around. The police were there earlier, but I wanted to check things out for myself."

"Because you thought you could find something they missed?"

"I did find something." Now it was Adam who glanced around. He seemed to take note of the customers and then studied the street. Nikki followed his gaze, almost expecting to see the panel truck parked at the curb or a tall, muscular man in a hoodie watching the shop. She detected nothing out of the ordinary, but her apprehension heightened as she turned back to Adam.

"What did you find?"

His gaze on her seemed even more intense. Relentlessly dark and unfathomable. "Remember earlier when I asked about the significance of the number forty-seven? You implied it meant something to Dr. Nance."

"Yes. It was the year he was born. 1947."

"That's it?"

"As far as I know. Why?"

He explained about the tilting-at-windmills phrase Dr. Nance had used during their last phone conversation, the copy of *Don Quixote* he'd found on the table next to the recliner and the rolled note that had been tucked up in the spine of the book.

Nikki listened, fascinated. "That doesn't sound like something Dr. Nance would do. He was never the cloak-and-dagger type. Anyway, how could he know you'd go to his cabin, find the book and put two and two together with what he'd said on the phone?"

Adam's focus never wavered. "Maybe he was banking on my abilities as a detective. Maybe someone else is, too."

Nikki leaned in, eyes wide. "You think someone is trying to stop you from looking into Dr. Nance's death?"

"Maybe someone is trying to stop you, too."

She suppressed a shiver. "I wish you hadn't said that."

"It had to be said. If someone is watching your house, you need to be careful."

"Why would someone consider me a threat? I'm not even the one who performed the autopsy."

"You were close to Dr. Nance. Someone might assume he confided in you."

Nikki fell silent as a million thoughts raced around in her head. *Could* she be a target? It seemed far-fetched, but wasn't she the one who'd had doubts all along about cause of death? All signs pointed to drowning, but after that long in the water, it was impossible to determine whether or not he'd been held under.

The images in her head were chilling. "We have to tell the sheriff everything. He needs to know. It could affect the direction of the investigation."

"I won't keep him in the dark," Adam said. "But I'm not backing off, either."

"He's not going to like a parallel investigation," Nikki warned.

"I wouldn't, either, in his shoes. But Dr. Nance left a note in that particular book for me to find. I think forty-seven means something other than his year of birth. I don't yet know the significance, but I have to assume he left other clues. I may be the only one who can find them." He paused, studying her features as if trying to assess her reaction. "As the county coroner, you're entitled to investigate as you see fit in order to establish cause, manner and circumstances of death."

Her gaze narrowed. "What are you getting at?"

"It would make my job easier if we worked together. Operating in an official capacity would open doors that I would otherwise have to kick in."

Nikki was taken aback by the proposition. "Are you suggesting I hire you on as another investigator?"

"You can call me your assistant, if that would make the arrangement more palatable to county officials."

"Whatever the title, that's a pretty bold request, considering I know nothing about you."

He removed a card from his pocket, jotted a name and number on the back and slid it across the table. "If you have any doubts about my credentials, call this man. He's been my unit commander for the past three years. He'll vouch for me."

She picked up the card and glanced at the name. "If you're that highly regarded by the police department, what are you doing down here?" She instantly regretted the question. "I'm sorry. That was stupid. You're here because Dr. Nance asked you to come."

"It's a little more complicated than that," he admitted. "The details aren't important to this case. Just give the lieutenant a call and let me know what you decide. You and Dr. Nance were close. You must want to find out what happened out on that lake as much as I do."

She slipped the card in her bag and nodded. "I'll give it some thought."

FOR THE REST of the day, Nikki ran errands and performed chores around the house, throwing herself into task after task so that she wouldn't have time to dwell on Dr. Nance's death, let alone the possibility that he'd been murdered. Or that she and Adam Thayer had somehow ended up in the killer's crosshairs.

No matter how hard she tried, though, she couldn't get their conversation out of her head. Teaming up with an outsider to investigate a beloved citizen's death wouldn't sit well with the local authorities. The last thing she wanted was to get on Tom Brannon's bad side. However, Adam had made a valid point. If the note Dr. Nance left in the spine of *Don Quixote* was a clue to whatever he'd discovered before his death, then Adam might be the only person who could find the other pieces of the puzzle. He might be the only one who could put it all together.

There was a reason he'd been asked to come down here. Dr. Nance could have gone to Tom Brannon or to her with his concerns, but he'd turned to Adam Thayer instead. Nikki couldn't dismiss her mentor's final request any more than she could disregard her own instincts. An accidental drowning was hard for her to accept even though the autopsy had produced no evidence to the contrary. She intended to go over the results again to see if anything had been missed, and she would hound the lab until the toxicology screen was completed. If Dr. Nance had discovered something sinister that had cost him his life, she needed to keep digging until she exposed the truth, even if it meant putting her own life at risk. She owed him that much.

But the possibility of a physical confrontation with an unknown suspect wasn't something she took lightly. As coroner, she'd been involved in any number of suspicious death investigations, but she'd never felt threatened, and her house had never been watched, so far as she knew. Dr. Nance's death was different. It felt personal.

Nikki thought about the gold watch from his late wife that had been taken from his house years prior to his death. One thing seemingly had nothing to do with the other, but she wasn't so sure anymore. After everything that had happened, it was getting harder to swallow as coincidence the discovery of that stolen timepiece in her secret hiding place. Maybe something nefarious really had been going on in Belle Pointe for years, but what? And where did Nikki and her missing journal fit into the mystery?

No one in town had been closer to Dr. Nance than Dessie Dupre. More than an employee, she'd been his friend and confidante and had kept his household running smoothly for three decades so that he'd been free to concentrate on his beloved hospital and clinic. As devastated as Nikki was by the loss of her mentor, she could only imagine what Dessie must be feeling.

It was time to go see her. Nikki had been putting off the visit, knowing how many memories would be stirred once she set foot in that house. Like Dr. Nance, Dessie had taken Nikki under her wing, assigning her little odd jobs around the house to earn spending money while coaxing her out of her shell. The least Nikki could do was offer condolences in person and maybe in the process find out if Dessie knew the whereabouts of Dr. Nance's journal. Dessie had always been very protective of his personal time and space. Maybe she'd feel more comfortable opening his study to a search by someone that she knew would treat his private domain with the utmost respect.

Nikki waited until twilight when the air had cooled before walking the few blocks over to Dr. Nance's neighborhood. She hoped any friends and neighbors who'd stopped by during the day would be gone by then.

Turning up the tree-shaded street, she paused on the sidewalk to admire the rambling one-story ranch that he and his wife had built before her death. He'd lived in that house alone for over three decades. Dessie had occupied the garage apartment at the back of the property for most of those years.

A light shone from the French doors in Dr. Nance's study, as if Dessie had somehow intuited Nikki's visit. Or maybe she'd just forgotten to turn off the light. The rest of the house was dark.

Accustomed to letting herself in through the back gate, Nikki walked up the driveway and stepped through into the lush garden, lifting her gaze to Dessie's apartment. All the lights were out there, too. Maybe she'd gone to stay with her sister for a few days. Understandable. The phone and doorbell would be ringing constantly since news of Dr. Nance's death had traveled through town. In Dessie's current state, she probably found it difficult to deal with all those sympathy calls and visits while coming to terms with her personal loss.

Nikki had started to leave when the sound of music registered. She thought at first the jazzy notes were drifting over the tall brick wall that enclosed the backyard, but then she realized the soft beat came from the large patio at the rear of the house. She heard muted voices then and the sound of water splashing in the pool.

She eased along the walkway until she could see around the corner of the house. Then she stopped short. A man she didn't know bounced lightly at the end of the diving board. The pool and garden lights had been turned off, casting the backyard in deep gloom. From his silhouette, Nikki could tell he was a big man, tall and broad-shouldered. Athletic. His presence in Dr. Nance's backyard was a shock. That he was stark naked was an even greater jolt.

The board popped as he bounced higher and then dived. He swam underwater to the shallow end and then rose, flinging water from his hair as he walked unself-consciously up the steps. He casually reached for a towel and wrapped it around his waist as Dessie emerged from the house. Nikki's first instinct was to call out a warning, but then she saw that Dessie wore a swimsuit. A sheer sarong covered her hips and floated about her slender legs as she sauntered up to the man in the towel.

Nikki froze, flabbergasted by the scene before her. She told herself to go back out the way she'd come in. Her presence was obviously an intrusion. But she stood rooted to the spot, unable to look away no matter how many ugly names she called herself.

Dessie poured drinks from an icy pitcher and the two clinked glasses. Then the man bent to adjust the speaker volume, filling the night with that hypnotic beat.

"Turn that down," Dessie scolded. "What will the neighbors think if they hear music over here and Dr. Nance not even in the ground yet?"

The man laughed softly, deeply. "That wall is nearly

a foot thick, darlin'. No one will hear a thing. But even if they do, who cares? You don't have to worry about the neighbors anymore. You don't have to worry about what anyone thinks, least of all that crazy old man you had to clean up after."

"Don't talk about him like that. Dr. Nance was always good to me."

"He took advantage of your generous nature. Paid you chicken feed for all that cooking and cleaning, and him sitting all that time on a fat ol' bank account. But we don't have to talk about him tonight or ever again. This place is yours now, babe, or soon will be. Your pool. Your backyard. You can do whatever you want." He ambled up behind her and kissed the back of her neck, swaying against her to the beat of the music.

Her head lolled against his shoulder as her hips moved with his. "You're bad for me, Clete."

He untied the sarong and let it fall in a silky puddle at their feet. "How bad?"

She sighed. "So bad I ache."

His towel came next as he pulled her against him. "Let's get in the water."

"No, Clete, don't!" she protested as he tugged her toward the pool. "I just had my hair done. People will be stopping by after church tomorrow and I need to look my best. Like it or not, I still have obligations."

"What about your obligation to me?" he murmured as he enticed her toward the steps.

"I shouldn't…"

"Oh, you should, darlin'. You really, really should…"

Nikki backed away then, tripping in her haste to get away and then pausing for a moment to make sure she hadn't been detected. The music covered her retreat. She used the seductive cry of the jazz horns to flee through the garden gate. Closing the latch with a faint click, she slipped down the driveway to pause yet again on the sidewalk to stare back at the house.

The sexy siren she'd seen in the garden just now was a far cry from the demure, steadfast woman who'd served her tea and cookies on the front porch, who'd cooked and cleaned and tended to Dr. Nance's every need for nearly thirty years without ever once complaining.

Nikki tried to cut her some slack. Everyone grieved in his or her own way. Dr. Nance would probably be the first to applaud Dessie for getting on with her life.

But what about this Clete person's claim that the house was now Dessie's to do with as she pleased? How did either of them know the provisions of Dr. Nance's will?

This is none of your business, Nikki.

It was and it wasn't. Dessie's love life might be off-limits, but as the Nance County coroner, she had an obligation to gather as much information as she could before reaching a conclusion as to the cause of death. Dr. Nance's journal might be invaluable in determining his frame of mind, but there was a proper way to go about obtaining it. For all she knew, the journal might already be in police custody.

Nikki told herself to turn around and head back home. Dessie had done nothing wrong. She was entitled to her privacy. Entitled to mourn Dr. Nance's death or celebrate his life in any way she saw fit.

Instead of retreating, Nikki turned to sweep her

gaze over the street and the neighboring houses before cutting across the grass to the end of the porch. The blinds in Dr. Nance's study hadn't been drawn all the way, giving her a glimpse inside. It was just as she remembered. So nostalgically familiar, she almost expected to see Dr. Nance seated behind his desk, surrounded by his books and keepsakes.

Nikki glanced away as a fresh wave of grief washed over her. She had no right to be here, but she *needed* to be here.

She tried the latches on the French doors, not surprised to find one of them unlocked. Despite his affluence and position, Dr. Nance had never been a stickler for security. He'd always seen the best in people.

Slipping inside, Nikki stood with eyes closed as she drew in the familiar scents of leather, furniture polish and the ubiquitous undercurrent of peppermint.

From inside the study, she could barely hear the music outside. She couldn't hear voices at all, or the subtle lap of water against the pool steps. She was grateful for the silence. She didn't need *that* image in her head.

Moving silently across the room, she scanned the bookshelves, appreciative as always of the variety of her mentor's reading material. A few of his favorites had been grouped separately from the others. Perusing those titles was bittersweet. They were some of Nikki's favorites, too. She and Dr. Nance had shared a love of reading, particularly the classics. She'd always admired his insatiable curiosity. No matter his age or success, he'd never tired of learning.

She left the books and moved to the rear window to

glance out. She could glimpse the garden and part of the pool from that vantage, but she didn't see Dessie or her companion. She could no longer hear the music, either. Her gaze lifted to the darkened garage apartment. Maybe they'd gone upstairs.

Turning away from the window, she hurried to the desk, checking the drawers and then the credenza, but the journal was nowhere to be found. Maybe it was in Dr. Nance's bedroom or his office at the clinic. She'd check with Dr. Wingate first thing Monday morning.

Heading for the French doors, she stopped in her tracks and slowly turned back to the bookshelves. One of the titles in Dr. Nance's favorites pile suddenly leaped out at her: *The Old Man and the Sea.*

He'd lent her a paperback edition not long after her mother had left town. Nikki had finished the book in two nights and then they'd sat out on the front porch discussing the themes and motifs. Truth be told, she'd been a little bored by the story and had paid scant attention then to the life lesson Dr. Nance had intended to instill. Later, especially in med school, she'd understood only too well the importance of never giving up in the face of defeat.

As the memories flooded over her, she retraced her steps across the room and plucked the thin novel from the shelf, glancing through the pages and then reading a passage here and there until something else came back to her. Something that had been nipping at the fringes of her memory. Now she flashed back to their final conversation when she'd run into Dr. Nance unexpectedly in town. What was it he'd said to her about his upcoming fishing trip?

Sure you won't humor an old man and come with me? This time next week we can be out to sea, not a care between us. Might even go out deep enough to catch a big blue.

A big blue. A marlin. The fish from Hemingway's tale.

Nikki's heart thudded as she thumbed back through the pages. Had Dr. Nance left a clue for her?

She took the book over to the lamplight and sat down behind the desk, examining the worn binding carefully. A tiny piece of paper had been stuffed up in the spine.

Voices sounded nearby and she rose to check out the window before realizing someone was coming down the hallway toward the study. She only had time to grab the book and dive underneath the desk before the door opened and someone came inside.

"I told you, Clete. I've been all through this room. It's not here."

"I know what you said, babe, and I believe you. But another set of eyes can't hurt."

"I just feel bad, pawing through his things like this. He always valued his privacy."

"The man's dead. He won't mind." A pause. "Did you leave that lamp on?"

"It's on a timer."

"Let's hope no one saw it from the street. Last thing we need is somebody dropping by with another greasy casserole."

"Then turn off the light and let's go back outside," Dessie said nervously.

"In a minute, darlin'. Is there a safe in here?"

"Not that I ever found."

"You checked all the desk drawers? The credenza? The bookshelves? We can't leave any stone unturned. You know how important this is."

Dessie suddenly sounded annoyed. "I've taken this study apart and put it back together a dozen times, just like I've done to every other room in this house. If there was anything to find, I would have come across it by now."

"I don't mean to be a pain," he said in a placating voice. "It's just...we've come this far. We can't be too careful."

"Clete—"

"What is it, babe?"

Nikki couldn't see either of them from her hiding place. She tried to picture the scenario. The man's voice was closer. He sounded as if he stood on the other side of the desk, but Dessie's voice came from across the room, as if she were hovering on the threshold, hesitant to enter Dr. Nance's sanctuary.

"I just had an awful chill," she said.

"It's the AC. It's always cold inside after a swim."

"It's not the air-conditioning. Something's wrong. I can feel it. Someone's been in here." Nikki heard the soft slap of her flip-flops as she entered the room. "If I didn't know better, I'd swear Dr. Nance was here."

"There's no such thing as ghosts," Clete said.

"I'm not so sure about that. I've felt a presence in this house ever since they found him."

"Now, don't you go getting spooked on me, Desiree Dupre. Eye on the prize, remember? In another few weeks, we'll be sipping mojitos on a secluded beach in the Caribbean. No worries, no nosy neighbors. No one around for miles. Clothing optional, of course."

Another silence followed by a rustling sound.

"Stop it, Clete. Not in here," Dessie whispered. "Let's go back up to my apartment."

"Whatever you say, babe. Just let me have a quick look—"

He moved around the desk. In another moment, he'd pull back the chair and spy Nikki. She had no excuse for being inside Dr. Nance's office. If she'd been able to justify her visit, she wouldn't be hiding underneath the desk.

She held her breath and clutched the book. The chair squeaked as he rolled it back. He was right there in front of her—

The doorbell sounded and he paused. Dessie hurried over to the French doors to glance out on the porch.

"It's that woman again." Her soft drawl hardened unexpectedly with contempt.

"What woman?"

"Lila Wilkes. I told you about her. She's already been by once today to talk about the funeral. I tried to explain to her that I need more time, but she won't leave me alone."

"Tell her there won't be a funeral. Tell her it was Dr. Nance's last wish."

"That won't stop her. She'll insist on some kind of memorial service, with or without my help."

"Then let her have at it. That's what she really wants, isn't it? To be in charge? It'll be one less thing you have to worry about."

"I guess, but Dr. Nance never had much use for

Lila Wilkes. It doesn't seem right, letting her have the final say."

"Dessie, Dessie. How many times do I have to say it? Charles Nance is no longer your concern. Let the old biddy have her fun."

The bell pealed again, sounding more insistent this time. Nikki could imagine Lila Wilkes on the porch, thumb pressed to the button as her brow furrowed in determination.

"She must have seen the light from the street," Dessie said. "I should have thought to turn off that timer."

"Too late now. Go see what she wants and then send her on her way. I'll turn out the light when I'm finished in here."

Nikki tracked the sound of Dessie's footfalls to the hallway door. "Make sure the blinds are drawn so she can't see you from outside. And for God's sake, be quiet until she leaves."

Clete moved away from the desk. "You sure you don't want me to come with you?" he teased. "I've always had a way with widows."

"Lord help me. Last thing we need is for her to get an eyeful of you."

He laughed seductively.

A note of fear crept into Dessie's voice. "I'm serious, Clete. You keep your distance from that woman. She may be the town do-gooder, but she's also got a big mouth."

Dessie's footsteps receded down the hallway, leaving Nikki alone in the room with Clete, whoever he was. She was still holding her breath, still clutch-

ing the book as she drew herself up into a tight ball.
Clete moved back around the desk and opened the
top drawer. He rummaged through the contents, then
closed the drawer softly and turned to the credenza,
where he rummaged through more drawers. Finally, he
gave up, turned off the lamp and left the room.

Nikki waited for several minutes before she scrambled from her hiding place and slipped out one of the
French doors. The evening was still hot and steamy.
Sweat trickled down her spine as she jumped off the
porch and crouched in the bushes, giving Lila Wilkes
enough time to exit before venturing into the moonlight. She was just about to move away from the house
when a slight sound startled her back into the shadows.

Lila slipped along the porch, glancing behind her toward the front entrance before easing up to the French
doors to peer in. Then she turned to scan the landscap-
ing and the street beyond. Nikki kept low, but for a moment she was certain the woman had discovered her.
Lila's keen gaze seemed to vector in on the very spot
where Nikki huddled. She even came to the edge of
the porch and peered down into the shrubbery.

"I know you're in there," she said softly.

Nikki hunkered lower.

"You rascal, you. Letting everyone think you're
dead."

What the—

"Come by the house when you're finished gallivant-
ing. I'll give you some tuna. You'd like that, wouldn't
you?"

A meow sounded from deeper in the bushes. Nikki

didn't move even when she felt something soft rub up against her leg.

"Here, kitty, kitty, kitty. Come out and let me see you."

The cat didn't budge. Instead, he pressed closer, gazing up at Nikki in the dark with wide, glimmering eyes.

"Have it your way," Lila muttered as she turned back to the French doors. "But sooner or later, I'll catch you. I always do," she added in a whisper.

Chapter Eight

Adam sat on the deck, watching Dr. Nance's cabin across the lake. He'd been out there since early evening, staring into the horizon as the colors shifted and the shadows cast by the pine forest lengthened. The water grew black as the sunset faded, and for a few breathless moments, heavy darkness descended until the moon rose above the treetops to cast a misty glow over the eerie landscape.

Somewhere downstream, the bellow of an alligator joined the background cacophony of the bullfrogs and whip-poor-wills and the eerie cry of his grandmother's roosting peafowl. With nightfall, the mosquitoes came out with a vengeance. Adam sprayed his ankles with repellent and then got up to wander down the wooden steps to the dock.

The johnboat bobbled gently against the tire bumpers, tempting him to climb in and motor across the lake to have another look inside the cabin. But if someone else watched and waited, he didn't want to scare that person away. He'd been on enough stakeouts to learn the value of patience.

He sat down in one of the bolted chairs and stretched

his legs in front of him, settling in for a long night. Folding his hands behind his head, he relaxed into his mission. Given free rein, his thoughts drifted back to his earlier conversation with Nikki Dresden. He hadn't been able to get a good read on how she'd taken his proposal. Not surprising, since he didn't know her that well. At least, not this version of Nikki Dresden. But the old Nikki Dresden? The dark, dramatic teenage Nikki Dresden who'd dressed in black and claimed as her safe haven the tumbledown ruins of a former psychiatric hospital? *That* Nikki Dresden he knew only too well.

He wondered how surprised—or upset—she'd be to learn that he'd found her journal that summer while searching through the Ruins looking for clues to Riley Cavanaugh's disappearance. His first thought when he'd pried up the loose floorboard and uncovered the notebook was that a former mental patient had left it behind. The writing was deep, despondent and hauntingly beautiful. It wasn't until he'd come across a passage about Riley's kidnapping that he realized the diary belonged to Nikki Dresden, the enigmatic girl with dyed black hair and soulful eyes.

He'd kept reading, justifying the invasion of her privacy by telling himself he might learn something that could lead him to the missing girl. He'd heard the rumors by then. The whispers of a satanic cult that had implicated Nikki and her friends. He'd found nothing, of course. The Belle Pointe Five were innocent in the kidnapping, but he wondered if the secrets and confessions that Nikki had poured out on the pages of her journal still haunted her at times.

He figured she'd gone up to the Ruins two nights ago to collect that notebook. Why else would she have pried up the loose board? Why else would she have been so flustered when he found her kneeling on the floor? Sure, the discovery of Dr. Nance's watch had been a shock, but the realization that someone had taken her journal must have been a thunderbolt.

Adam could only speculate as to why she'd left it there all those years. She must have had her reasons. Was she home tonight, wondering who'd taken it? Worried if it would turn up when she'd finally been embraced by her hometown?

Or was she fretting about their earlier conversation? Contemplating his proposition?

Did he occupy her thoughts the way she was beginning to his?

His phone dinged an incoming text and he glanced down. Nikki Dresden was so much on his mind he almost expected to see a message from her. Stephanie's name at the top of the screen stopped him cold. His ex was about the last person he wanted to hear from tonight, but she'd always had an uncanny instinct for catching him at a low point.

She wrote: I guess you're surprised to hear from me.

An understatement. He stared at the screen, waiting for the old anger and bitterness to surface, but he felt strangely calm. Not indifferent, not yet, but he didn't feel the need to respond or retort. He just wanted to go back to the solitude of his thoughts.

A few seconds ticked by before another message dinged.

We need to talk, Adam. Can I call you? It's important.

His thumb hovered over the screen but he still didn't answer.

I know you're reading this. I'm going to call.

Still so sure of herself.

"Adam?"

The voice coming so unexpectedly out of the darkness startled him. He pivoted to glance up the steps where a silhouette hovered.

He rose. "Nikki?" How easily her name slipped from his lips. How natural his name had sounded on hers.

"Yes, sorry. I didn't mean to startle you."

"No, it's okay. I didn't hear you drive up."

"I parked out on the road." She came down the steps then, deliberately moving from the shadows so that he could see her more clearly.

She was dressed as usual in jeans, T-shirt and sneakers, but there was something different about her tonight. Her hair seemed glossier in the moonlight, her lips fuller, her eyes more luminescent. She wore an air of mystery like a subtle perfume. Or was that just his imagination playing tricks? Was he subconsciously trying to prove to himself he was over Stephanie Chambers by acknowledging his attraction to Nikki Dresden?

"I wasn't trying to sneak up on you or anything," she said as she tucked back her hair. The other side fell like a shimmering curtain over the side of her face.

"The driveway is so overgrown, I wasn't sure I could get through."

"It's tricky," he said. "I need to do some pruning with a chain saw and machete, but I've grown accustomed to the privacy."

She nodded absently. "It is private. I almost missed the house. Anyway, I knocked on your door. When you didn't answer, I took a chance you might be down here." Her gaze dropped to the phone he still clutched in his hand. "I hope I'm not interrupting."

As if on cue, the ringtone jangled. He didn't bother glancing at the screen.

"You can get that if you need to," she said. "I'll wait for you up at the house."

He pressed the decline button and slipped the phone in his pocket. "It's not important."

She came down the rest of the steps. "I should have called first. I didn't even think."

"No, it's fine. I'm not busy. I was just sitting here watching Dr. Nance's cabin."

The dock rocked gently as she stepped onto the platform and edged along the railing to peer across the darkened lake. "Have you seen anything?"

"All clear so far." He moved up beside her, glancing at her profile and thinking to himself that he shouldn't be so happy to see her. He was restless enough tonight to want to act on his attraction, but cautious enough to know that a rebound hookup probably wasn't such a great idea. Assuming, of course, she'd even be open to his company.

The insistent chime of his ringtone was like a splash

of cold water. He took out his phone, pressed the decline button once more and silenced his ringer.

Nikki turned to glance up at him. "Someone's persistent. Are you sure you don't want to get that?"

"I'm sure." He leaned his forearms on the railing as he stared out over the water. Across the way, he could just make out the silhouette of the cabin. Moonlight glinted ghostlike from the windows. Something stirred inside Adam. Excitement? Anticipation? The thrill of the hunt? He'd gone too long without a case to solve. Too long without getting laid, too, he reckoned. He turned back to Nikki. "What brings you out here tonight? Have you considered my proposal?"

"No," she said bluntly. "I mean, yes, I've thought about it, but I haven't had time to make a decision. Something else has happened that I think you should know about."

He straightened at the somber note in her voice. "What is it?"

"I went to see Dessie Dupre a little while ago." She told him about her visit to Dr. Nance's house, the shock of finding a nude man on the diving board and the overheard conversations by the pool and in the study. Her brow creased as she relayed the evening's events. "It was surreal. Dessie seemed so different. Younger and more vibrant. *Womanly*, I guess would be the word."

"You don't have any idea what she and her companion were looking for in the study?" Adam asked.

"Not a clue, although at first, I thought they might be searching for Dr. Nance's journal since that's why I was there. But in hindsight, I wonder if they were looking for a copy of his will. The man, Clete, seemed certain that Dessie would inherit the house and maybe a good deal of cash. He said in a few weeks, they would be sipping drinks on a secluded beach in the Caribbean. Of course, if they already know Dessie is inheriting the house and some money, I don't know why they'd need to find his will."

"I take it you don't know this Clete person?"

"I've never seen him before. He's a big guy, though. Tall with broad shoulders. Looks like he works out a lot. It occurred to me that he might be the person who attacked you last night. You said the assailant was strong, right? I didn't get a good enough look to see if Clete had bruises, but I had the impression he was considerably younger than Dessie. She seemed…smitten."

Adam smiled at her word choice. "Smitten?"

Nikki shrugged. "Besotted. Enamored. Whatever you want to call it, she was clearly under his spell."

"It shouldn't be too hard to find out who he is," Adam said. "I'll do some digging. If we can connect him to that old panel truck, we'll be in business."

"I wouldn't count on that." She raked back her hair, letting moonlight settle on her cheekbones. "He didn't seem the type to drive a truck. I'm guessing he's more the sports car type. Something flashy. Although I admit I'm basing that on a very brief, overheard conversation."

"Sometimes that's all it takes. I wouldn't discount your instincts."

She stared down into the water as the night sounds vibrated around them. The lake seemed almost mystical tonight. Adam studied her profile, wondering how he could have ever found her less attractive than his former fiancée. Stephanie was as hot and sultry as a summer day, but Nikki Dresden belonged in moonlight.

She turned and caught him staring at her. Their gazes held for a moment before she glanced back out at the water.

"Clete isn't the only reason I drove out here tonight," she said.

Adam leaned against the rail and turned into her. "No?"

She paused as if detecting something in his voice that unsettled her. "I found something in Dr. Nance's study tonight. Maybe something more important than his journal. I only thought to look because of what you'd told me earlier about the note rolled up in the book spine. I remembered what you said about Dr. Nance's use of the phrase 'tilting at windmills' during your last conversation and how he left that copy of *Don Quixote* in the cabin for you to find. It was a clue that only you would recognize. Earlier I found a clue that only I would recognize."

His scalp prickled a warning as he ran a hand through the clipped strands. "Go on."

"He left a copy of *The Old Man and the Sea* in a prominent position on one of his bookshelves. That story was important to both of us. I read it as a kid and we talked about it a lot. The last time I saw him, he invited me to go fishing with him in the Gulf. He said we might go out deep enough to catch a big blue. A marlin is the fish—"

"I'm familiar with the Hemingway story," Adam said. "Did you find anything inside the book?"

"Yes. A rolled-up note in the spine just like the one you found. Only this one had 14 written on it."

"Do you have the note?"

"Not with me. I put it back in the book and locked it in my desk drawer at home."

"Does that number mean anything to you?"

She shook her head helplessly. "I've racked my brain. I went through all the birthdays and anniversaries that may have been important to Dr. Nance. Nothing. But earlier, Clete asked Dessie about a safe. She said she didn't know of one in the study, but that got me to wondering if these numbers could be a combination. Or a password."

"That's as good a guess as any at this point," Adam said.

She sighed. "It's just a guess, though. For all we know, the numbers could be nothing more than a manifestation of Dr. Nance's delusions. If his mental faculties were slipping, as some people seem to think, he could have imagined this 'dark thing' and then left cryptic clues that don't actually mean anything to anyone but him. Under ordinary circumstances, I can't imagine him behaving so mysteriously. If he thought something was wrong, he would have gone to the police."

"Unless he was worried that whatever he'd discovered might fall into the wrong hands before he had a chance to verify his findings. Anyway, he did go to the police. He called me."

Her gaze faltered. "I meant the local authorities."

"I know. And I understand what you're saying about his mental state, but both things can be true. He could have uncovered something criminal even as he realized dementia was taking hold. Bottom line, I didn't imagine the man at the cabin who shot at me. Nor did I dream up the driver who tried to run me down today. Something is definitely going on in Belle Pointe."

She drew a breath. "I know."

"And it seems as if Dr. Nance was counting on the two of us to figure it out."

He saw her shiver in the dark. "With what we have to go on so far, that's a tall order."

"I've never backed away from a challenge. I get the sense that you haven't, either."

"I can be stubborn," she admitted. "Those numbers keep bugging me. Forty-seven and fourteen. Four-seven-one-four. Could be the last four digits of a phone number. Or maybe even a Social Security number."

"Anything's possible. Without additional information, trying to find meaning in those numbers is like looking for the proverbial needle in a haystack. Right now, we need to find that panel truck and figure out who this Clete guy is. Those could be solid leads."

She nodded. "Something else happened tonight. It's probably not important, but I found it interesting just the same. Lila Wilkes showed up at Dr. Nance's house while I was hiding underneath the desk in his study."

"Who's Lila Wilkes?"

"She's a local woman," Nikki said. "A lot of people around here think of her as their guardian angel. Or maybe 'an angel of mercy' would be a more apt description. She spends a good deal of her time tending to the sick, especially the ones who are housebound. She's been a godsend to the elderly. Takes them shopping, ferries them to doctor's appointments and whatnot. Wherever they need to go."

"Sounds like a regular Mother Teresa," Adam remarked.

"I don't know that I'd go that far, but she certainly fills a need in our community. I think you've met her. Average height, slim build. Gray hair cut in a short bob. In her late fifties, I'd guess. When she dropped by to visit me yesterday, she mentioned that she'd run into you in town the other day. You seemed to have made an impression on her."

"I think I know who you mean. Asks a lot of questions. Likes to hear herself talk."

Nikki nodded. "That would be Lila. Until tonight, I'd always bought into the saintly image that everyone seems to have of her."

"What happened tonight?"

"Dessie said she didn't feel right letting Lila plan a service for Dr. Nance because he hadn't thought too highly of her."

"Did Dessie say why he felt that way?"

"No, but it really surprised me because Lila told me the other night that Dr. Nance is the one who persuaded her to come to Belle Pointe in the first place. Of course, that was a long time ago."

"How long?"

"Decades. She's been here for so long that people forget she wasn't born here. I probably wouldn't have given any of this a second thought if I hadn't seen her skulking around outside Dr. Nance's study."

That caught Adam's interest. "What do you mean by skulking?"

"Sneaking around on his porch, peering into his study. I'm one to talk, since I did the same thing myself. Still, there was something odd about her behavior. On my way home, I remembered something my grandmother once said about her. 'Butter won't melt in that woman's mouth.' My grandmother wasn't a kind person, but she was more often than not a sound judge of character."

"What are you saying?" Adam asked. "You think this Lila Wilkes had something to do with Dr. Nance's death?"

"The notion seems utterly insane. I can't think of a single motive she'd have. But at the very least, I find it curious that her image may not be as squeaky clean as I've always been led to believe."

"A lot of things about Dr. Nance's death—about this whole town, for that matter—are curious," Adam said.

Nikki's tone turned grim. "That's putting it mildly. So, where do we go from here?"

"Not much more we can do until morning. It's a little late to go out looking for that truck. We could go back over to the cabin and search through the other books. Another note could give us some clarity. Are you up for that?"

"Yes, of course. Whatever it takes."

"Give me a minute to lock up the house and grab some flashlights." He paused. "Are you sure about this? Things got a little dicey the last time I was over there."

She straightened from the railing. "You don't think

the person who shot at you last night will come back tonight, do you?"

"Not likely. But if he does, I'll be prepared this time." Adam was already climbing the steps when she called his name softly. He turned back. "Yeah?"

"I keep thinking about how it might have happened. The drowning, I mean. If someone took him out in the boat, pushed him in and held him under..." She trailed off. "I can't get that image out of my head."

"We'll find out what happened," Adam said. "I gave my word to Dr. Nance and now I'm giving it to you. We're in this together, okay?"

NIKKI WATCHED THE lake with a brooding frown. A mild breeze blew off the shimmering water, cooling the sultry air as it stirred the honeysuckle that grew at the top of the embankment. It was a beautiful summer evening, but her head was filled with violent images. She didn't want to picture Dr. Nance's last moments, but how could she help it? Had his killer somehow lured him out in the boat? Had he tried to fight off his assailant, or had the attack caught him by surprise?

Maybe his death had been nothing more than a tragic accident. There was no concrete evidence to the contrary. But even after the autopsy, too many questions lingered. Why had he abandoned his trip to Houston? Why had he asked Adam Thayer, a Dallas police detective, to come down and help make sense of what he'd found? What *had* he found?

Nikki dealt with death day in and day out, but no one close to her had ever been murdered. Who would want to kill a small-town doctor who'd devoted his life to helping the people in his community?

Money seemed the most likely motive, but Nikki couldn't bear to contemplate such a cold-blooded act. That Dessie Dupre might somehow be involved was even harder to accept. The woman had always seemed devoted to Dr. Nance, and in return, he'd given her a comfortable home and a steady income for most of her life. But the promise of easy money could change a person. So could the influence of another. Who was this Clete person, and how and when had he come into Dessie's life? Had the planning of Dr. Nance's death taken months or had it been a spur-of-the-moment scheme?

As tempting as it was to pile the blame on a stranger, Nikki reminded herself of the presumption of innocence. Other than his size, there was no reason to suspect Clete was the man who had shot at Adam at the cabin last night or tried to run him down earlier in town. There were a lot of strong guys in the area. As for Dessie…she was a good, kind and gentle person. Nikki refused to believe otherwise, no matter what she'd witnessed earlier.

She'd been so caught up in an endless spiral of suspicion and denial that it took her a moment to realize a light had come on inside the cabin. Her heart thudded as she straightened. She couldn't see anyone moving about, but that light hadn't come on by itself.

She heard Adam on the steps behind her. "Someone's over there," she said when he came up beside her.

He peered across the moonlit lake. "Did you see anyone on the water?"

"No. I would have heard a boat unless they were using oars. I didn't see headlights, either, although the trees are so thick, I could have missed them." She turned anxiously. "Should we call the police?"

"Whoever is over there could be long gone by the time a squad car gets out here. I say we stick to our plan and go check things out for ourselves."

Apprehension skittered along her backbone. "What did you mean when you said you'd be prepared this time? Are you armed?"

"Yes."

She hesitated, then nodded. "I guess that's a good thing. Should I drive the boat or would you rather I keep lookout?"

The question seemed to surprise him. "I have to say, you're a little more gung ho about this than I would have expected."

She laughed awkwardly. "I'm not gung ho. I'm pretty nervous, if you want to know the truth, but we have to do whatever is necessary to find out what happened to Dr. Nance."

He hesitated. "I doubt we'll run into trouble, but just in case, keep your head down. Don't let adrenaline make you do something foolish."

Nikki climbed down into the boat, taking the center bench while Adam cast off and took the tiller. The small rig put-putted away from the dock. On any other night, Nikki might have enjoyed the leisurely trip across the lake, but now she sat hunched forward as if she could somehow will more horsepower into the motor. The moon was up and full. Anyone looking out a window or from the top of the embankment could easily spot them. The term "sitting ducks" came to mind. She glanced around uneasily.

Once they were far enough out, she could trace the outline of the bridge where she'd first seen Adam all those years ago and, farther down the lake, what she imagined to be the looming silhouette of the smoke-stack and the crumbling roofline of the Ruins. She remembered seeing him there, as well, could even recall a word or two of their brief conversation. He'd tried to draw her out, but she'd been suspicious of his interest and protective of her privacy. She hadn't wanted to take the chance that he might see right through her.

The images of him were so vivid to her now, highlighted by the lingering horror of that terrible summer, she wondered why she hadn't recognized him straightaway. Everyone who had lived through Riley Cavanaugh's disappearance, even if in a peripheral way, would always be connected by that tragedy.

"You okay?"

His voice sounded hushed in the darkness. She glanced over her shoulder. "I'm fine. Oddly enough, I was thinking about Riley."

"What about her?"

"I was thinking how you can meet someone you think is a stranger, but then you find out that the shared experience of her disappearance connects you."

"That's pretty deep."

Too deep for their current situation, she supposed. *Keep your eye on the prize, Nikki.* That phrase made her think of Clete. Who was he and what the hell had he done with the Dessie she'd known for most of her life?

"We're almost there," Adam said. "I'll cut the engine as soon as we get a little closer."

She turned back to scour the water as they approached the bank. "I don't see a boat at the dock. They must have come by car."

He shut off the engine and guided the prow toward the bank. Nikki ducked to avoid the trailing moss. They both climbed out and pulled the boat aground, and then Adam handed her one of the flashlights. "The moon is so bright, we shouldn't need them, but just in case."

Nikki tucked the flashlight into the back of her jeans and nodded. They moved quickly along the bank to the steep wooden steps, pressing into the shadows as they climbed up to the deck. Adam peered through one of the glass doors, then slipped to the other side and motioned for Nikki to step up to the window.

She pressed herself to the wall and then took a peek inside. A woman stood at Dr. Nance's desk, rifling frantically through the drawers.

Chapter Nine

The intruder had her back to the deck, but Nikki immediately recognized the tall, elegant form and the chic, cropped hair. Dr. Patience Wingate's movements were uncharacteristically hurried and desperate. Nikki had never known her to be anything but cool, calm and somewhat arrogant.

She was so taken aback to find Dr. Nance's partner going through his desk that she stepped from her hiding place without thinking. Adam motioned her back, but it was too late. Dr. Wingate must have heard a slight sound, for she whirled, clearly shocked to find someone peering in through the window.

Casting a wary glance around the space, she strode across the room to draw back the French door.

"Dr. Dresden! What are you doing here?" Caught in what for anyone else would have been an awkward situation, she quickly assumed her normal, haughty mask, placing one hand on the door and the other on her hip as she regarded Nikki with open suspicion.

Nikki smiled, allowing nothing more than mild curiosity to seep into her tone. "Dr. Wingate! My goodness, you gave us quite a start. We saw the light from across the lake. We thought someone must have broken into Dr. Nance's cabin."

"That's preposterous. I didn't break in."

Her defensive tone caught Nikki off guard. "No… of course not. But we didn't know it was you."

"How *did* you get in?" Adam asked casually as he stepped forward. He seemed relaxed and, like Nikki, outwardly displayed benign curiosity, but she could detect tension in the set of his features and in the way his gaze scouted their surroundings.

Dr. Wingate cocked her head slightly. "I'm sorry. Who are you?"

Nikki hastened to make the introductions. "This is Adam Thayer. He's a Dallas PD homicide detective."

"Is that so?" She didn't sound at all impressed by his credentials, but Nikki caught the flash of something that might have been confusion in her gray eyes. Or was that fear? "What on earth are the two of you doing out on the lake at this time of night?"

"Detective Thayer has a house just over there." She gestured toward the opposite bank. "He came down to do some work on the place and has accepted a temporary assignment with the Nance County coroner's office." She could feel Adam's surprised gaze on her in the dark, but she refused to glance his way. "We're looking into Dr. Nance's death."

"What's there to look into?" Dr. Wingate demanded. "I was told his boat overturned and he drowned. Was I misinformed?"

"There are still a lot of unanswered questions," Nikki hedged.

"What kind of questions?"

"For starters, you never told us how you got in here." Adam nodded toward the open desk drawers. "Or what you're looking for."

She gave Nikki an irritated look. "Dr. Dresden, is this really necessary? I've already spoken to Sheriff Brannon."

Nikki forced a sympathetic note in her voice. "I know this is hard, considering how close you were with Dr. Nance. It's difficult for me, too, but we'd really appreciate a few minutes of your time. The more information we can gather, the easier it will be for my colleagues and me to reach a consensus on cause of death."

Dr. Wingate sighed in frustration. "I don't see this as anything but a monumental waste of my time, but if you must know, Charles gave me a key to the cabin years ago so that I could come out on weekends when we—when I needed a quick getaway. As to what I'm looking for, I'm here on clinic business."

"What kind of business?" Adam asked.

"I need to make certain that any medical records Charles may have removed from the clinic have been appropriately secured under current privacy rules."

"Do you mind if we come in?" Adam asked.

"Why would you need to come in?"

"This conversation might be easier if we all just relax," he said.

"I suppose, but only for a minute or two." She grudgingly stepped back from the door. "It's getting late. I'd like to finish my task and get back to town."

"We won't keep you long." Adam motioned for Nikki to go ahead of him and then he closed the door.

Dr. Wingate turned, clearly displeased by this turn

of events and looking as if she wanted to boot them both right back out the door. "I honestly don't know what more I can tell you."

"Did you locate the files you were looking for?" Adam asked as he glanced around the space.

She hesitated. "I never said I was looking for specific files."

"You must have reason to believe that some are missing if you're going to this much trouble."

She walked back over to the desk and rested a hip against the corner, a fifty-something woman of supreme confidence and little patience. Her personal style was sophisticated and spare, and yet there was a hint of sensuality in the way she leaned back on her hands and gazed across the room at them. "The clinic is fully computerized. We don't even ask patients to fill out paper forms anymore. Charles was a little slow to adapt to our new system. He preferred the old-fashioned method of file folders and color-coded tabs. He'd even go so far at times as to have his assistant print out files just so he'd have a hard copy to study. When he was finished, he'd return the file to his assistant for shredding."

"Sounds like a lot of extra work," Adam said.

"Whatever Charles Nance wanted, he usually got," she said with a trace of bitterness. She caught herself and shrugged. "He was the boss, after all. Anyway, his assistant came to me yesterday morning right after we heard the news. She said he'd requested several files a few weeks ago and never returned them for shredding. If those files were to fall into the wrong hands, the clinic could be subject to a number of costly fines and possibly the kind of lawsuits that could bankrupt us."

"Why did you think the files would be at the cabin?" Nikki asked.

"Because Charles came here before he died. And because we couldn't find them at the clinic or at his house. This was the last place I could think to look. I drove out the first chance I had to search."

"How many files are missing?" Adam asked.

"At least a dozen, some of them dating back years."

"Do you have a list of the affected patients?"

"I do, but I won't release that information without a court order. Besides, the names are unimportant. Patient privacy is all that matters."

Adam nodded. "Do you have any idea why he wanted the files?"

"Only that he told his assistant he was working on some mysterious project. I have no idea what that project might be, but then, we were all concerned about his behavior these past few months."

"Sheriff Brannon told me about some of the problems he'd had at the clinic," Nikki said. "Do you know if he underwent any cognitive testing?"

"Not that I'm aware. He knew something was wrong, though. At first it was small things like misplacing his keys and forgetting his phone. But the incidents grew progressively more serious. That's when I knew I had to step in. He was devastated, of course, but he understood. In some ways, he may even have been relieved that I'd forced the issue. He agreed to phase out his practice as soon as he returned from his trip."

"I wonder why he never mentioned anything to me about his impending retirement," Nikki said.

"Maybe he hadn't fully come to terms with it himself," Dr. Wingate suggested. "Charles was a very proud man, and the aging process took a toll."

"When did you last speak to him?" Adam asked.

"The day before he left on his trip. He was in good spirits, considering. He looked forward to reconnecting with some of his colleagues. He'd even planned a fishing trip."

"Why do you think he had a change of heart?" Adam asked.

"I have no idea. Maybe he got confused and came to the first familiar place he could think of."

"You're a full partner in the clinic?"

"No. Dr. Nance kept fifty-one percent when he allowed me to buy in. He wasn't one for relinquishing control." There was that hint of bitterness again.

"What sort of arrangement do you have in place in the event of a principal's death?"

She straightened. "How can that possibly be any of your business?"

"I understand it's an uncomfortable question," he said. "But as Dr. Dresden mentioned, the more information we can gather, the easier it will be to determine what happened."

"Charles drowned. That's what happened. Nothing I can tell you will change that tragic fact."

"He drowned," Adam agreed. "But we're not convinced it was an accident."

His bluntness drew a gasp. She gazed at them in shock. "You can't possibly think Charles was murdered. He was beloved by the whole town."

"Maybe not by everyone," Adam said. "His popularity aside, he was a successful doctor with a flourishing practice. When looking for motive, it's always helpful to figure out who had the most to gain from his death."

Patience Wingate's expression hardened as she rose from the desk. "Are you suggesting *I* had something to gain?"

"Of course not," Nikki said quickly, but Adam merely shrugged.

"If the partnership was designed so that the surviving partner inherits the practice, then yes. You'd have a great deal to gain from Charles Nance's death."

"Wow," NIKKI SAID AS they went down the steps together. "You really got under her skin. Did you see her face before she ushered us out?"

"She looked pretty upset."

"Upset? If she'd had a gun, she might have shot you on the spot."

"Comes with the territory," Adam said. "I don't feel I've done my job unless I've ruffled a few feathers."

"Rest assured, you excel at what you do," Nikki replied dryly. "Seriously, though, I find it hard to believe that Patience Wingate would be capable of murder. She's a doctor, and a very good one, from what I hear, despite her abrasive bedside manner. Dr. Nance would never have allowed her to buy into the clinic if he didn't think highly of her abilities."

"You think doctors—even good ones—are incapable of taking lives?" He sounded amused. "I don't know, Dr. Dresden. She seemed wound pretty tight to me."

"Really? She's always struck me as very cool and

analytical. Not the type to get her hands dirty with homicide."

"Appearances are often deceiving," Adam said.

"So I've been told."

He paused halfway down the stairs and turned to her. She was a step or two above him so that they were standing eye to eye. The nearness quickened her pulse, but she told herself to settle down. If they agreed to enter into a working arrangement, it had to be temporary and remain strictly professional. She didn't need the kind of messy complications that seemed to follow a man like Adam Thayer. Maybe that was an unfair assessment since she'd known him for such a short time, but he'd been living on Echo Lake for little more than a week and already he'd been shot at, beaten up and nearly run down by an unknown driver, all while recovering from his previous gunshot wounds. Danger followed him, too, apparently.

"Think about it this way," he said.

"I'm sorry. Think about what?"

He gave her a quizzical look. "You okay?"

"Yes. I lost my train of thought for a moment."

"We were talking about Dr. Wingate and whether or not she might be capable of murder."

"Right."

"I say, who better than a medical doctor to commit the perfect homicide? She has access to drugs. She has a key to Dr. Nance's cabin, possibly to his house, and she was familiar with his schedule and habits. That gives her means and opportunity. If she stood to gain from his death, there's a motive. I'll be interested to see what the tox screen reveals."

"After that long in the water? Possibly nothing," Nikki reminded him.

"We'll see."

She glanced back at the cabin. The light had gone out, but she could make out Patience Wingate's silhouette at the window. "She's still inside. I think she's watching us."

"Probably wants to make sure we leave." He looked tense and pale in the moonlight. Deadly, Nikki thought with a shiver. In more ways than one. "Maybe she didn't have anything to do with Dr. Nance's death, but she's hiding something."

"How can you be so sure? She seemed forthcoming about her reason for searching the cabin."

"Was she?"

"You didn't buy the story about the missing files?" Nikki asked.

"Oh, I think she was looking for those files, all right, but maybe not for the reason she gave us. Do you happen to know the assistant she mentioned?"

"Darla? She's been with Dr. Nance for years. She and I went to high school together. We're on friendly terms these days, but we aren't friends."

"Do you think she'd be willing to do a favor for Dr. Nance's protégée?"

"You mean me?" Nikki frowned. "What kind of favor?"

"We need to get our hands on a list of those patient names."

"Why? What do you think is in those files?"

"I don't know, but Dr. Wingate doesn't strike me as the type to do her own grunt work. If she were only worried about HIPAA violations and patient privacy, why didn't she give the key to the assistant and send her out here to search the cabin? Why wait until tonight if she learned about the missing records yesterday?"

"I assume you have a theory."

His gaze flicked past her up the steps, probing the shadows behind them. Gooseflesh prickled at the back of her neck.

"What is it? Did you see something?" she asked anxiously.

"No, but we shouldn't stand out here any longer. We're too exposed. Let's head back to the boat."

She hurried down the steps after him. "Okay, but what's your theory?"

"Maybe there's something in those medical records she doesn't want anyone else to see."

"Like what?" They were at the edge of the lake now. The water lapped softly against the bank.

"I don't know. Evidence of malpractice. Kickbacks from drug or insurance companies. Could be anything. When Dr. Nance called me, he said he'd pulled files and made notes. It was all there in black and white, but he needed my help to make sense of what he'd found."

"You think he meant these files?"

"Seems a reasonable conclusion."

"But he never said anything about Dr. Wingate, right? He never even mentioned criminal activity. He said something strange was going on in Belle Pointe. Something dark. That could mean anything or nothing at all. I feel I need to point out that you're building a case against Dr. Wingate from little more than thin air."

He nodded his approval at her rebuke. "It's good to play devil's advocate. Keeps me honest. But I'm not accusing Dr. Wingate of anything. Yet." He slapped a mosquito at the back of his neck as if to emphasize his point. "You have to admit, as a suspect she ticks a few boxes. I think a deeper dig is warranted."

They fell silent at the sound of an ignition turning over. Nikki cocked her head toward the steps. "Sounds like she's leaving. Shouldn't we go back up? We didn't get the chance to conduct our search. Maybe we can find another piece of evidence."

"Let's leave it for now. We've pressed our luck enough for one night. I'll come back over in the morning and take another look."

They pushed the boat back into the water and hopped in. Adam steered them away from the bank and out into the moonlight. Nikki had to resist the urge to glance over her shoulder. Maybe it was her imagination, but she sensed invisible eyes upon them and she couldn't help wondering if someone watched from the shadows at the top of the embankment. Or through the night vision scope of a rifle.

She kept her eyes peeled and breathed a sigh of relief when they drifted up to the dock on the opposite side of the lake. Adam shut off the engine and they both climbed out. She stood on the dock keeping watch while he tied off.

"See anything?" He moved up beside her at the rail.

"No. Dr. Wingate is probably halfway back to town by now. Everything seems quiet enough. But…" Nikki trailed off on a shiver as she wrapped her arms around her middle.

"What's wrong?"

"You don't feel it?" When he shook his head, she turned back to the water. "I have the strongest sensation that someone is watching us." She peered across the lake, trailing her gaze all along the bank and tree line. Or was the watcher behind them? She glanced over her shoulder, suppressing another shiver as she tried to calm her jitters.

He braced his hands on the rail as he scanned the opposite bank. "Someone could be out there. Or you could be experiencing the aftermath of an adrenaline rush."

"I know the difference."

He straightened. "Then don't discount your instincts. If we're starting to rattle some cages, things could get dangerous. Don't let down your guard."

"I won't. But let me play devil's advocate one more time and remind you that we don't even know for certain we're dealing with a homicide. We don't know anything yet."

"That's not true. We know that Dr. Nance asked me to come down here and look into something he'd found. We know he had a change of heart about his trip to Houston and that he left clues in book spines. We know that little more than twenty-four hours after his body was found, someone shot at me at his cabin and tried to run me down on a busy street. Granted, none of that adds up to murder. Not yet. But we both need to stay vigilant. Until we know more, we should consider anyone connected to Dr. Nance a suspect, and that includes Dr. Wingate and Dessie Dupre."

"It's just so disconcerting to think that someone

I've known my whole life could be a stone-cold killer," Nikki said. "I keep going over what you said about motive. Who stood to gain from Dr. Nance's death? I wonder if there's any way we can find out the details of his and Dr. Wingate's partnership agreement."

"That could be difficult, but see if the assistant knows anything when you talk to her about the files. Be discreet. We don't want to tip our hand too soon, much less cross the line into harassment."

"I'll do my best."

He ran a hand through his short hair, a habit he seemed to have when he was agitated or pensive. Funny how she was already starting to recognize his mannerisms. She wondered what he had picked up about her.

The moonlight seemed to deepen his gaze. "Can you think of anyone who would have a key to Dr. Nance's cabin besides Dr. Wingate? I left the door to the cabin open last night while I was inside, but I got the feeling the suspect, whoever he was, knew his way around."

Nikki shrugged. "He was always having work done at the cabin or at his house in town. He had a thing about maintaining his properties. He could have given a key to a worker or repairperson, I suppose. Maybe your shooter is the same thief who took the gold watch and hid it at the Ruins."

"Why would he leave it there all those years?"

"Panic. Fear of getting caught. All the pawnshops in the area would have been alerted by the police. Maybe once the heat finally died down, he'd forgotten about it. My point is, a leopard doesn't change his spots. By the time you went to the cabin, word was already out about

Dr. Nance's death. Maybe your attacker went out there to see what he could steal. Maybe he thought he'd find drugs. Who knows? When he saw you, he freaked."

"This guy didn't seem the type to freak," Adam said.

She slid her gaze over his bruised face. "Do you have another explanation for the watch?"

"Yes, but nothing I care to share at the moment."

"That doesn't seem fair. Didn't you say we're in this together?"

He hesitated. "Give me a day or two. Like I said, I need to do some digging."

Nikki couldn't leave it alone. "You don't think Dr. Wingate took the watch, do you?"

"She's hiding something, but I doubt it was that watch."

Nikki grew quiet and pensive as she listened to the night sounds all around them. A breeze rippled through the leaves like the trickle of a stream. The bullfrogs and whip-poor-wills were still out, their serenade mournful and nostalgic from the shadows. On such a soft summer night, it seemed obscene to Nikki that they spoke almost casually about the possibility that Dr. Nance had been murdered by someone he trusted, someone she might have passed on the street that very day.

Adam was still watching her in the moonlight. Intently, she thought. She wondered if he felt the attraction, too. Had he experienced the same pull of destiny that had caught her off guard at the Ruins that first night? Or was there a darker explanation for his keen scrutiny? He'd told her he remembered the rumors and whispers about the Belle Pointe Five. He said he never believed them, but a part of him must have wondered about her. Maybe subconsciously he was still wondering. All it took was a single niggling doubt to make him ponder the possibility, no matter how far-fetched, that she may have been the one to take that watch. Or worse. Anyone who had been connected to Dr. Nance should be considered a suspect, he'd said. Did that include her? Why else would he be so evasive now?

The very notion turned her blood cold and threatened to erode the trust and camaraderie they were building. She told herself he wouldn't have asked to work with her if he thought her capable of murder, but what better way to keep a close eye on a suspect than to put yourself in her orbit?

Nikki had tried to walk away from her past the day she left for college, but in the space of a heartbeat, the old doubts and insecurities returned with a vengeance, along with her defenses. She reminded herself she was no longer that girl. No one side-eyed her anymore when she walked down the street. People no longer speculated about those vile rumors. Why borrow trouble?

"Is there anyone else you can think of who would have benefited from Dr. Nance's death?" Adam asked.

She tried not to read anything into the question. "Not really. His wife has been dead for years and they didn't have any children. According to Lila Wilkes, he has a nephew in Atlanta and some cousins scattered about, but he wasn't close to any of them."

"Do you know if he was ever sued for malpractice? Or threatened by a patient or bereaved relative? Someone out for revenge, maybe."

"Not that I'm aware. Belle Pointe is a small town. I'm sure I would have heard through the grapevine if there'd been any trouble of that nature. Given Dr. Nance's standing in the community, it would have caused a scandal."

"What about business deals that might have gone sour?"

She started to relax again. His questions were routine and entirely expected. She was making too much of his elusion. "I wouldn't know anything about that."

"Romantic entanglements?"

She frowned. "You're the second person who's mentioned something like that to me today. Tom Brannon suggested that Dr. Nance and Dessie might have had a relationship at one time. I don't think it likely. I never saw anything but friendship and respect between them. Maybe I wasn't looking. Even now, it's hard for me to picture Dr. Nance in a romantic relationship. Or even on a date, for that matter. I always assumed he was still madly in love with his wife."

"That's a little naive," Adam said. "I got to know him pretty well before my grandmother died. He talked a bit about his wife. He was barely forty when she passed, still a young guy. I'm sure he loved her deeply, but he didn't seem like a man stuck in the past to me. I had the impression he'd moved on a long time ago. He even talked about a couple of his relationships that had ended badly."

That stopped Nikki cold. "Relationships? Plural?"

"Apparently he got around."

She stared at him in shock. "You're telling me Dr. Nance was a player?"

Adam grinned. "He didn't put it quite like that. He did say there was one involvement in particular that he wished he could take back."

"Don't mind me," Nikki muttered. "I'm just a bit speechless at the moment."

"Because he was human?"

"Because I'm apparently oblivious. Did he happen to mention a name?"

"He was too much of a gentleman for that."

"Did he say why he regretted the relationship?"

"She became obsessive. When he broke things off, she stalked him for a time. I got the sense she made his life pretty miserable."

Nikki stared at him wide-eyed as something fell into place. "Wait. You think this woman, whoever she is, took his watch, don't you?"

"It's a theory."

"You think *she* killed him?"

"I'm not willing to go that far out on a limb yet."

Nikki was glad for the darkness that covered her sheepish expression. Talk about jumping to conclusions. Of course Adam didn't suspect her. She needed to get over herself. "I don't know what to say. First I find out Dessie Dupre has a secret life and now Dr. Nance." She tucked back her hair, a habit she had when distressed or confused. "I can't believe he told you all those intimate details about his life. He never even told me he was retiring."

"Sometimes it's easier to talk to an outsider. I wouldn't take it personally."

"I'm not." But she couldn't help feeling remorseful and perhaps just a tiny bit jealous. Why hadn't Dr. Nance come to her when he needed help? Why hadn't he told her about all the problems he'd been having at the clinic? Had she been so wrapped up in her own life that he'd felt she didn't have time for him? She shook her head. "He had a stalker. I'm still blown away by that. I wonder what else he didn't tell me."

"That was a long time ago," Adam said. "Maybe you'd already gone off to college when it all went down. Besides, everyone keeps secrets."

Nikki glanced away, discomfited once more by the intensity of his gaze. She wanted to ask about his secrets, but she didn't want him probing into hers. "I should get going."

"You don't need to rush off."

"I'm not rushing. It's late and I've had a long day. I'm sure you have, too."

"Nikki?"

Her heart thudded at the way he said her name. Butterflies quivered as their gazes connected. "Yes?"

He hesitated for the longest moment. "Be careful going home. Maybe I should follow you back into town."

Was she disappointed or relieved at the way the evening was ending? "I appreciate the offer, but it's not necessary. I'll be fine. We'll talk soon, okay? Tomorrow is Sunday. I'll be home most of the day. Maybe we can get together and hammer out the details of our arrangement. That is, if you were really serious about working together."

He nodded. "I'll call you."

She could feel his eyes on her as she started up the steps. She told herself to be cool and keep walking.

Don't turn around. Don't let him know you're interested. It was way too soon to let down her guard.

She made it all the way to the top of the stairs before she glanced back.

Chapter Ten

The next day, Adam drove into town on a mission. The streets were quiet, and the hush deepened as he left the business district behind and entered one of the upscale neighborhoods that bordered the downtown area. The houses here were older and eclectic, ranging in styles from colonial to Victorian to sprawling ranches. Many of the homes displayed fresh face-lifts, the cosmetic renovations complementing the meticulous lawns and lush gardens.

Locating Dr. Patience Wingate's address, he drove by her house twice to make sure he had the right place. Then he pulled to the curb at the end of the street and lowered his window, letting the warm, fragrant breeze drift through his vehicle.

He wouldn't be able to stay in one spot for too long. In a quiet neighborhood like this, he'd get noticed. Sunglasses and a ball cap provided only so much camouflage. He wasn't even sure what he hoped to accomplish staking out her place. *Call it another hunch.* He'd been certain the evening before she was hiding something and the feeling had only strengthened overnight, so much so that he'd awakened that morning with a sense of urgency.

Finding her address hadn't been a problem. He'd been prepared to call in a favor from one of his remaining friends at the Dallas PD, but a simple internet search had yielded the necessary results. He'd packed a small cooler and grabbed some snacks before heading into town, and now he settled down with a bag of peanuts as he kept his eyes peeled for curious neighbors.

One hour went by and then two. He drove around the block and changed parking spaces, finding an inconspicuous spot between two other vehicles that he hoped would offer some cover. It was starting to get uncomfortably warm in the car. Adam grabbed a bottle of water from the cooler and tossed out the last of the peanuts. A flock of blackbirds descended from the power lines to gobble up his leftovers.

Around ten, Dr. Wingate came down the walkway to collect the newspaper at the curb. She scanned the street and then quickly retreated to the shade of the porch to peruse the headlines. Adam zeroed in on her with his binoculars. She looked as if she were dressed to go out. Smart black slacks, sleeveless white blouse. Sandals. Gold jewelry. Classy and expensive, he thought. He tried to imagine her luring Dr. Nance out on the lake and then pushing his head underwater, but the visual didn't click with the fastidious woman he observed through the lenses.

She took a call while outside. The conversation seemed to upset her. She paced the length of the veranda as she talked, pausing at one point to search the street. He slumped down in the seat as she glanced his way. Her gaze lingered for a second too long before she whirled abruptly and paced to the other end of the porch. She ended the call and went back inside, leaving the newspaper pages to flutter in the breeze.

Another hour went by, and as boredom set in, Adam was reminded of how much he hated surveillance. By noon, the neighborhood had become more active with weekend gardeners, dog walkers and people returning home from church. He took a break and drove a few blocks over for some takeout, returning a little while later to yet a different parking space and a different view of the house. All seemed quiet.

He ate his burger and sipped his Coke while he decided what to do next. The stakeout had been a long shot. Surveillance sometimes took days if not weeks or months to yield results. If she really was concealing nefarious behavior, she wasn't likely to tip her hand on a single Sunday morning. Still, beneath that reserved demeanor, Adam had sensed desperation the night before. Whatever was in those files, she seemed anxious to recover and shred the information before anyone else saw it. If he'd read her right, she wouldn't wait long to make her next move.

He was sitting there contemplating what that next move might be when the garage door lifted and a dark blue BMW backed down the driveway and out into the street. Quickly, he stuffed his food wrappers in the take-out bag, started his engine and then waited until Dr. Wingate had made the first turn before he pulled away from the curb.

The neighborhood was basically a large circle with a series of shorter streets connecting the two sides.

With only one way in and one way out, Adam gave her plenty of time to exit before he followed her onto a busier thoroughfare. She made two stops in town, one at a coffee shop with a drive-through window and the second at an ATM machine.

It was early afternoon by this time. The hot sun streamed in through the windshield. He adjusted his cap and cranked up the AC as he kept a safe distance. Tailing someone without being detected was a lot harder than the movies made it seem, especially in broad daylight on a Sunday afternoon. The lighter traffic didn't afford much coverage. He dropped back even farther, taking a chance on losing her rather than being spotted.

She drove all the way through town and turned onto the highway, heading toward the lake. Adam thought at first she might be going back out to Dr. Nance's cabin, but she didn't make the turn onto Lake Road. Instead she kept going, picking up speed on the two-lane blacktop until he had no choice but to fall back out of sight. If he tried to keep pace, she would surely pick him up in the rearview mirror.

Ten miles out of town, he was certain he'd lost her. He accelerated, passing an elderly couple in a sedan and a pickup truck emitting black smoke from the tailpipe. He had no idea where she might be going. There wasn't much to see out this way except for pine trees and swampland. They were literally in the middle of nowhere. Maybe she had relatives in the area. Didn't seem likely, but Adam doubted she was out for a casual Sunday afternoon drive.

He slowed, contemplating whether to turn around

and head back toward town or keep going. He still had plenty of time to touch base with Nikki. He'd been looking forward to their next meeting all morning. Maybe his anticipation was a little too keen, he thought.

His attraction to the coroner unnecessarily complicated things. He wasn't the type to drift from one romance into another. Until Stephanie Chambers came along, he hadn't considered himself the relationship type at all, could never have pictured himself settling down with a wife, kids and a house in the burbs. She'd been his one exception, a risk he'd felt was worth taking, and look how that had turned out.

He didn't fool himself that he was over the breakup. Not completely. He still experienced twinges of bitterness and regret now and then. Those pangs were getting fewer and farther between, but that didn't mean it was time to jump back into deep water. Not with all his baggage. The smarter move was to chill for a while—

There!

He caught a glimpse of the BMW flying down a dirt road, dust clouds swirling in its wake. He braked and pulled to the shoulder, waiting until her vehicle disappeared around a bend before he made the turn and followed her down the narrow lane.

Pine trees rose all around him, the feathery bowers reaching across the road to block all but slivers of sunlight. Kudzu had invaded the ditches, crawling up light poles and creeping along fencerows until Adam's world narrowed to a thin green tunnel. A quarter of a mile in, he came to a metal gate. A hand-painted sign nailed to one of the posts proclaimed Junkyard. Another warned Trespassers Will Be Shot and a third read simply Dogs.

Adam reversed down the road until he found a place to pull off in the trees, concealing his vehicle as best he could. He got out and walked back to the unlocked gate, slipped through and then paused to note the quiet of the countryside. He heard the distant sound of barking dogs before a shouted reprimand silenced them. He checked his permitted firearm, tucked it back in his jeans and set out.

Keeping to the side of the road where the shade was deepest, he eventually emerged at another gate, through which he glimpsed the dark blue sedan. He left the road and hunkered at the edge of the woods while he scouted the property.

Junked cars of every make and model, some squashed flat and piled high in precarious stacks, littered the remote property. A forest of rusted appliances sprouted near the fence, along with various pieces of farm equipment. A small metal building with a covered porch had been erected to the right of the gate. Adam guessed the rudimentary structure served as an office and the larger building next door housed tools and equipment.

At the back of the property, he could see the tin roof of a house peeking through the trees and wondered if that might be Dr. Wingate's ultimate destination. Despite the presence of her car, he was hard-pressed to imagine she had business with a junk dealer.

Catching wind of a new scent, the dogs grew frenzied. Adam didn't think they could get through the fence, but he scrambled back a few feet anyway. The snarling rose to a ferocious crescendo until a brawny man came out on the porch and shouted a sharp command. The dogs quieted immediately. The man's height and physique brought to mind the shooter at the cabin. Adam could still feel the explosive impact of that large body bulldozing into him on the dock. The guy came to the edge of the porch and surveilled the immediate area before disappearing back inside.

Since the dogs hadn't rushed toward the fence, Adam figured they must be tied up or penned. He cut along the tree line until he spied a chain-link fence enclosing the area between the two metal buildings. He could make out two sleek silhouettes pacing back and forth, but the German shepherds were either so disciplined or so cowed they didn't react even though they had to be aware of his approach.

Adam told himself to call it a day and head on back to town. Nothing more he could do here. But he couldn't silence the nagging voice in his head that prodded him to move in closer even as the scar across his scalp prickled a warning. He kept low as he moved out of the trees, quickly climbing over the fence and dropping with a soft thud on the other side. The heads in the pen came up and he heard a growl. Giving the enclosed area a wide berth, he ran across the open yard and took cover at the back of the building, inching around the corner toward a window.

He flattened himself against the metal structure, waiting to see if the dogs reacted to his nearness. Nothing. No more barking. No sound at all except for the muted voices inside. Adam eased up to the window. Despite the sunlight reflecting off the glass, he noted two people inside. Dr. Wingate stood with her back to the front door, allowing Adam to glimpse her profile. She appeared to be arguing with the guy who had come out moments earlier to quiet the dogs.

He placed his hands on the desk between them and leaned toward her in a menacing fashion. Dr. Wingate held her ground for a moment before taking a step back. The man straightened and laughed.

Another brief argument ensued before Dr. Wingate withdrew a thick envelope from her purse and flung it toward him. The man caught the packet, opened the flap and riffled through the contents, all the while keeping a close eye on his companion. Seemingly satisfied with what he found, he sat down in his chair and propped his feet on the desk.

Their business apparently concluded, Dr. Wingate turned toward the door and Adam ducked, retreating to the back of the building, where he peered around the corner to observe her exit. She strode down the driveway, threw back the gate and climbed into the BMW, slamming the door soundly before she swung the car around and accelerated down the dusty road.

Adam checked his surroundings, readying himself to make a dash for the fence, when he spotted something familiar to his left. The old panel truck was nearly hidden between two rows of smashed vehicles. He started forward and then halted once more.

Slowly, he turned. The dog pen was empty.

NIKKI SPENT MOST of the morning weeding and trimming in the garden, but after a few hours the heat drove her back inside. She showered and changed clothes, then puttered about the house at loose ends. She thought about calling Adam to see if he wanted to meet, but didn't want to appear too eager. Which really didn't make sense, considering their current situation. They were both professionals, and if she intended to hire him on as an investigator for the coroner's office, then they would need to keep in close contact. She couldn't be worried about what he might or might not think every time she called him. She *shouldn't* be concerned about anything except the inquiry into Dr. Nance's death.

That all sounded well and good, but Nikki knew her personal feelings were going to complicate the arrangement. Deep down, her dark doppelgänger still lurked. A part of her would always be the insecure girl who had watched her mother drive away that day, knowing she hadn't been enough. Since that painful revelation, Nikki had done everything in her power to avoid feeling that way ever again. She'd put up barriers and kept to herself all through high school and college. Even now, she only casually dated. A few of her relationships had lasted more than a month, but when things got too serious, her first inclination was to bolt before she got hurt. Leave before she got left behind.

Something had happened on the dock last night with Adam. Something she hadn't been able to run away from, no matter how hard she tried to convince herself the sparks had been nothing more than the aftermath of an adrenaline rush. But it wasn't the physical attraction that scared her. It was the sense of something profound lurking behind the brief smiles and lingering glances that spooked her.

She couldn't help wondering what he would be like

in bed. After sex, how easy would it be for her to walk away?

That she even contemplated such a question was itself a warning. How masochistic would she have to be to get involved with a man who would leave town once the investigation was over or as soon as his old life beckoned?

They had a good thing going at the moment. They were on the same page regarding Dr. Nance's death. The lack of evidence tied Tom Brannon's hands to a certain extent, but Adam didn't have to concern himself with the rules and protocol that came with the county sheriff's badge. He was here temporarily, more or less a rogue investigator. Hiring him on at the coroner's office lent an air of legitimacy to his inquiries, but Nikki had no doubt he would pursue the truth with or without her help.

She wasn't one to give up, either, especially after having found a clue in Dr. Nance's study that could only have been meant for her. Together she and Adam would piece together what had happened on the lake the day Dr. Nance had died. Ask enough questions and sooner or later the truth would sort itself out.

To that end, Nikki decided to pay Dessie Dupre another visit. She wasn't sure how much she could get the housekeeper to divulge about her personal life. She'd done a good job of keeping her relationship with Clete a secret. Still, Dessie trusted Nikki, and with the right finessing, she might let something slip. Nikki hated the duplicitous nature of her visit, but as the coroner and Dr. Nance's friend, her first obligation was to justice.

Plus, calling on Dessie provided a convenient excuse to get out of the house and stop fretting about why Adam Thayer hadn't called.

See? This is why you don't get involved. This is why you keep your distance. Uncertainty breeds insecurity.

Shrugging off the tug of self-doubt, she called to make sure Dessie would be home and didn't mind company. The woman sounded so pleased to hear from Nikki that guilt dogged her all the way over to the house. She reminded herself yet again that no matter what she'd overheard, Dessie would never be a party to harming Dr. Nance. Having a boyfriend—even a smarmy one—didn't make her guilty of anything except possibly questionable taste.

A classic fifties convertible sat in the driveway when Nikki arrived. Sleek and about a mile long, it was an impressive vehicle even from a distance. She knew very little about the restoration of vintage automobiles, but it didn't take an expert to know that someone had dropped a fortune on that car.

The driver had left the top down, relying on the shade of an oak tree to protect the leather and burled wood interior from the sun. Nikki walked around the car, running her hand lightly over one of the fenders as she admired the mirrorlike finish. She didn't recognize the vehicle, but it seemed the kind of car that one of Dr. Nance's fishing buddies might own. Probably belonged to someone who had driven in from out of town to pay his respects. Even so, Nikki glanced over her shoulder at the house before snapping a shot of the license plate with her camera phone.

She climbed the porch steps and took a peek through

the side window as she rang the bell. As soon as she caught a glimpse of Dessie, she stepped back. The door opened and Nikki was at once drawn into a warm, motherly embrace. The residual scents of cinnamon and vanilla drifting out the front door took her back to her adolescence. The delectable aroma of Dessie's baking had always comforted her when the unpleasant combination of her grandmother's sharp tongue and the acrid odor of joint liniment had driven her out of the cramped house.

Dessie hugged her tight and then pushed her away, holding her at arm's length to search her face. "You look tired, sweetie. How're you holding up?"

"I should be asking you that question."

Dessie sighed. "I still can't believe he's gone."

"I know. It's been such a shock to everyone. I should have come sooner, but I—"

"Hush." Dessie gave her a little shake. "You don't need to apologize to me. I know you've had things to do, you being the coroner and all. I can only imagine how hard it must have been to see him like that."

"It was…difficult."

Dessie winced. "I don't know how you get something like that out of your head. Still, as awful as it was for you, it's been a comfort to me, knowing you were there with him. I knew you'd see to it that he was treated with the proper respect."

Nikki swallowed hard. "He was."

"I never doubted it for a second."

Nikki chose her next words carefully. "Actually, I did drop by last evening to see you. The lights were out. I thought perhaps you'd gone to stay with your sister."

Was that bewilderment or fear that flared in the woman's eyes? "Last evening, you say? What time?"

"Twilight. I walked over from my house."

"Did you ring the bell?"

"No. The lights in your apartment were off, too, so I figured if you were home, you were resting, and I didn't want to disturb you," Nikki lied.

Dessie paused as if to think back. "I may have been out by the pool. On hot evenings, I sometimes sit with my feet in the water and watch the sunset. I probably wouldn't have heard you come up if I had the radio on. But it really doesn't matter anyway. I'm glad you're here now."

Nikki managed a smile. Why she didn't just come right out and ask Dessie about her companion, she wasn't sure, but something warned her to proceed with caution. *Finesse, remember? Let her do the talking.*

It seemed wrong to manipulate a woman who had never treated Nikki with anything other than kindness, but she couldn't ignore what she'd seen and overheard. Dr. Patience Wingate wasn't the only person in Dr. Nance's life who had something to hide.

As if sensing Nikki's discomfort, Dessie squeezed her hand. "We're not going to get maudlin, you hear me? Dr. Nance would hate that. He'd want us to remember the happy times."

"I know. And I do have so many good memories of him here."

"I was just thinking earlier how the two of you used to sit out here as soon as it got dark, watching for lightning bugs. That was the start to every summer, seeing who could spot one first."

"You'd bring us sweet tea and gingersnaps. Sometimes you'd put on a record album from his old collection. I can still remember the sound of music drifting out through the open windows."

"After a while, he'd get to talking about his medical school days. Some of those stories would curl your hair. Like the time someone put a skeleton in his bed." She shook her head and chuckled. "I could just picture his face."

"He was a great storyteller," Nikki said. "And a very great man."

"Amen."

Dessie's smile turned reflective as she gazed out at the street, seemingly lost in the past. Nikki used the opportunity for a stealthy observation. Dessie was still dressed for church in a simple navy dress cinched at her narrow waist with a white belt. Her lips and eyes were subtly enhanced and she'd pinned back her thick curls with a mother-of-pearl comb. Nikki had always admired Dessie's gentle beauty. She wore her age well. Though she was in her fifties, her skin was still supple, her figure still trim, and only a few silver strands glinted in her hair. It was hard to reconcile the pretty, unassuming woman Nikki had known her whole life with the sultry siren she'd glimpsed poolside last evening.

She must have stared too long and too intently because Dessie's hand crept to her throat. "Goodness, Nikki. The way you're looking at me…is something wrong?"

Nikki caught herself. "What? No! I'm sorry. I was just thinking how pretty you look today."

Dessie's sad smile flickered again. "You've always been such a sweet girl. I never understood how your mama and daddy could take off and leave you the way they did."

"Apparently they needed more out of life than being my parents."

"Foolish, selfish people. But we won't waste another breath on that worthless pair." She took Nikki's arm and urged her toward the door. "Come on. Let's go inside, where it's cool. We've got a lot to talk about and there's fresh lemonade in the refrigerator. Plenty to eat, too, if you're hungry. We had a crowd after church, but everyone's gone, so we have the house to ourselves. Well, almost."

"You must have had your fill of company by now," Nikki said. "Are you sure you're up for another visit?"

"You're not company. You're family." Dessie pushed open the door, took a glance inside and then turned back to Nikki. "I should warn you that Dr. Nance's attorney is still here. He brought over some paperwork. Nothing to worry about. Just a little matter he's taking care of for me." Her fingers slipped again to her neckline as her gaze seemed to falter. "We're finished now and he was just leaving."

"I don't want to interrupt," Nikki said as she followed Dessie inside. She paused in the foyer. "I could come back later."

"You'll do no such thing. He'll want to say hello anyway. Dr. Nance always spoke so highly of you."

"Well, in that case…"

As always, the house was cool and spotless, a welcome refuge from the intense Texas heat. The furnishings were plush and comfortable, and the artwork covering the walls ranged from watercolors by local artists to framed snapshots of the surrounding countryside. Books were stacked neatly on shelves and on the coffee table. Nikki wanted to take a closer look to see if any of the titles stood out, but Dessie was already propelling her toward the kitchen.

"Talk about memories," Nikki murmured. "I've always adored this house. I used to think of it as my happy place."

Dessie squeezed her arm. "Dr. Nance would have been so pleased to hear you say that. It's a pity he and Miss Audrey were never able to fill it with the children they both wanted. Then losing her to cancer when she was still a young woman. Some things aren't meant to be, I guess. But despite all that heartache, he was a big believer in living life to the fullest. I never heard him complain once about his misfortunes. There's a lesson for all of us in that. Live each day as it comes. You never know what tomorrow will bring."

"That's true."

Nikki followed her through the dining room into the large eat-in kitchen, where a row of windows across the back of the house looked out on the pool. A man dressed in charcoal slacks and a white pullover was seated at the breakfast table with an open briefcase before him. He closed the lid as they entered and rose.

Nikki froze as he came forward, her pulse jumping

in agitation. She couldn't be sure, but she thought he might be the man she'd seen with Dessie last evening.

Wait a minute.

Dessie's creepy boyfriend was Dr. Nance's attorney?

...

Chapter Eleven

Dessie put an arm around Nikki's shoulders. "Mr. Darnell, I'd like you to meet Dr. Nikki Dresden. I'm sure you've heard Dr. Nance speak of her many times."

"I have, indeed." His smooth drawl was unmistakable. He extended his hand, and Nikki could do nothing but offer hers in return. "So many times, in fact, I feel as if I already know you, Dr. Dresden. Or may I call you Nikki?"

"Nikki is fine," she said stiffly.

"Cletus Darnell." He shook her hand firmly. "My friends call me Clete."

Somewhere in his late forties, he oozed a slippery charm with his easy smile and glib demeanor. He wore his dark hair slicked back from his face, highlighting blue eyes, thin lips and a hawkish nose. Handsome, Nikki supposed, if one overlooked the hint of smugness in that easy smile and the glint of cold calculation in those baby blues.

Remembering the unpleasant way in which he'd spoken about Dr. Nance last evening, Nikki slid her hand away. "Clete, is it? Dessie said you were Dr. Nance's attorney. I'm sorry, but I never heard him mention you," she said coolly. "What happened to Mr. Townsend?"

"He retired some months back," Dessie said. "Mr. Darnell took over his practice here in Belle Pointe. He also has an office over in Longview."

"You must be a busy man," Nikki murmured.

"Keeps me out of trouble." He flashed that charming grin as he reached inside the briefcase and extracted a business card. "Should you ever need my services."

"Thank you, but I have an attorney."

He shrugged. "Keep the card anyway. One never knows."

"One never does," she agreed, as she pocketed the card. "When did you say you took over Mr. Townsend's practice?"

"Last spring. The papers were finalized in May, to be precise."

"Funny, I don't remember seeing you around town. Is that your car in the driveway? Impressive. I'm certain I would have remembered seeing a vehicle like that on the streets."

"It's not my everyday ride," he explained. "I save it for special occasions."

"This is a special occasion?"

"It's a beautiful Sunday afternoon and I'm standing here with two lovely ladies, so yes. I would say this counts as a special occasion, the underlying reason for my visit notwithstanding." He sobered. "I am sorry for your loss. I know Dr. Nance thought of you as family. So does Dessie."

"Thank you," Nikki said. "We were both just saying what a great man he was."

"I didn't know him well, but I always enjoyed our interactions," Clete said. "He had some good stories to tell."

"When was the last time you saw him?" Nikki asked.

His gaze slid to Dessie and back. "I beg your pardon?"

"You said you enjoyed your interactions. That implies you met him more than once. I'm curious when you last saw him."

"He came into the office a few times after I took over the practice," Clete said. "I made the effort to touch base with all Mr. Townsend's clients, encouraging them to update their wills and so forth. You'd be surprised how many people neglect such things."

"I suppose it's understandable," Nikki said. "Being confronted with our own mortality isn't something most people enjoy."

"And yet as the county coroner, you confront mortality every single day. Automobile accidents, old age… even murder. I would imagine some of the more gruesome cases keep you up at night."

The statement was casually spoken, but Nikki could have sworn she heard a taunt in his tone. Or was it a subtle threat? She thought about the elusive shadow she'd glimpsed in her backyard during the storm the other night, followed by the lumber of an old truck out on the street. She doubted Clete Darnell had had anything to do with either, but she couldn't dispel her uneasiness. As Dr. Nance's attorney, he was privy to all manner of personal and financial material. Maybe he'd found a way to update that information and then had somehow wormed his way into Dessie Dupre's unassuming life.

Nikki gazed back at him. "Some cases do keep me up, particularly the ones with no easy answers. But I'm a light sleeper anyway. Even the sound of an old truck passing by on the street will sometimes rouse me."

A smile flickered even as his eyes narrowed. "Maybe you should consider moving to a quieter neighborhood."

Dessie had been standing silently listening to the back-and-forth, but now she said a little too briskly, "My goodness gracious. If this isn't the strangest conversation I've heard in quite some time."

"Yes. We do seem to have strayed a bit off course," Clete agreed.

Her smile looked strained. "Why don't the two of you have a seat? I'll get the lemonade."

"None for me," he said. "I should get going so the two of you can have a visit. I've taken up way too much of your time as it is." He turned to Nikki. "Normally, I wouldn't have asked to come by on a Sunday afternoon, but I was in town on other business, and seeing as how I'll be out of the office for a few days, it seemed a good idea to tie up loose ends. One less thing for Dessie to worry about." He opened the lid of the briefcase and removed a large manila envelope, which he placed on the table as Dessie brought over a tray. "Here are the copies you requested for your files."

Under normal circumstances, Nikki would probably have never noticed the way his fingers brushed against Dessie's and lingered. Or the way Dessie quickly snatched her hand away. But even without knowing what she knew, Nikki would have wondered about Clete Darnell's smirk.

"Thank you," Dessie said primly. "I'll be sure to put them in a safe place." She poured from an icy pitcher and handed Nikki a glass, keeping her head bowed to the task as if to avoid Clete's gaze. "Are you sure you don't want one?" she asked him.

"Now you're just tempting me," he teased. "How did you know old-fashioned lemonade is a particular weakness of mine in the summer? And yours looks especially mouthwatering. I suppose a little sip couldn't hurt."

His syrupy charm was lost on Nikki. She resisted rolling her eyes as she studied Dessie's reaction. Bright spots of color had appeared on her cheeks.

Then she switched her focus to Clete, annoyed to find that he had seated himself at Dr. Nance's usual place.

Dessie poured a third glass and took the chair opposite Nikki's. They sipped in silence, glancing at one another over the rims of their glasses. A more awkward or suspicious gathering Nikki could hardly imagine. She didn't want to picture Dessie and Clete together, but how could she not when her gaze kept straying to the swimming pool?

She couldn't grasp how someone like Clete Darnell had managed to sweep a sensible woman like Dessie Dupre off her feet. But then, maybe she didn't know Dessie as well as she thought she did.

"How did the two of you meet?" she asked.

Dessie glanced up in alarm. "What?"

"You said Mr. Darnell—Clete—is taking care of a personal matter for you. I assume Dr. Nance recommended him?"

"Actually, we met at church," Clete said.

"At church?"

"That's right," Dessie agreed. "I wasn't aware that he had taken over Mr. Townsend's business at the time. I didn't know who he was at all, in fact. We got to talking over potluck, and when I found out what he did for a living, I asked if I could come in and speak with him about a matter." She gave Clete a longing glance before she caught herself. She lowered her head and vigorously mopped up a ring of condensation with a paper napkin. "Finding out he was also Dr. Nance's attorney was just a happy coincidence."

I'll bet.

Clete folded his arms on the table and leaned toward Nikki. "Actually, it's fortuitous that you came over when you did. You've saved me another trip." He removed a letter-size envelope from his briefcase and slid it across the table to her.

"What's this?" she asked in surprise.

"A request that you attend the reading of Dr. Nance's will. It's ceremonial, of course. Probate is handled at the courthouse, but Dr. Nance had his own way of doing things. I've put it on the calendar for four o'clock on Wednesday afternoon at my office here in Belle Pointe. It seemed the most convenient time and place for everyone involved."

"Why would you want me there?" Nikki asked.

His tone was slightly chiding. "Oh, come now. As

close as the two of you were, it surely isn't a surprise to learn that he remembered you in his will."

"He did?"

"Though I feel I must caution against high expectations. People get their hopes up thinking a friend or family member has left them a sum of money only to realize their inheritance constitutes nothing more than a cherished antique or a sentimental keepsake."

Nikki's eyes burned as she picked up the envelope. "I don't know what to say. A keepsake would be all that I could ask for and more. But is this a normal time frame? Doesn't probate take longer? There hasn't even been a funeral yet."

"As I said, this is an unofficial ceremony and there's to be no funeral," he said. "Didn't Dessie tell you?"

Dessie's hand slipped back to her throat. "I'm afraid we haven't had a chance to talk about that yet."

Clete nodded almost imperceptibly as the two exchanged glances. "As per Dr. Nance's instructions, his body is to be cremated and his ashes scattered on Echo Lake. He didn't want a service of any kind."

"I see."

"He left everything spelled out," the lawyer added. "His wishes were explicit."

"You know how the man hated to be fussed over." Dessie couldn't quite meet Nikki's gaze.

"Well, if that's what he wanted," Nikki said, but she couldn't help wondering if those instructions had recently been fabricated as a means of facilitating a trip to the Caribbean. Or was there a darker purpose for a quick cremation?

"Now that we have that out of the way…" Clete shut

the lid of his briefcase and snapped the latches. "Thank you for the lemonade, Dessie. Uncommonly delicious, as always. And, Dr. Dresden… Nikki. It was a pleasure to finally meet you."

"Thank you again for coming by on such short notice," Dessie said. "Working on a Sunday really is going above and beyond the call of duty."

"Nonsense. I do what I can to help out. This is a stressful time for everyone who knew Dr. Nance. If I can make your life a little easier, then that's reward enough for me." He picked up the briefcase and stood. "If you have questions or require additional services, just let me know."

Dessie rose, too, smoothing the sides of her dress as if she didn't quite know what to do with her hands. "I'll see you out."

"No need. I know the way." The doorbell rang just then and he turned toward the foyer. "Another casserole, no doubt."

Dessie picked up the large envelope and slid it into a kitchen drawer before accompanying him to the front door. Nikki could hear the murmur of their voices as they walked through the house. She got up and peeked around the corner into the dining room and the foyer beyond. Dessie and Clete stood facing one another in the entrance. Dessie had her hand on his arm, her fingers lightly clutching as he bent to say something in her ear. He turned his head and caught Nikki's gaze a split second before she jerked back around the corner.

The look on his face…the flash of violence behind his eyes sent a chill up her spine. Just who the hell was this guy?

Heart hammering, she remained out of sight until she heard the front door open and a third voice chimed in. She couldn't be sure, but she thought the visitor might be Lila Wilkes.

Taking another quick glance around the corner, she hurried back into the kitchen and eased the drawer open to quietly extract the envelope. She undid the metal clasp, telling herself all the while that she was nothing more than a miserable snoop, spying on Dessie Dupre, of all people, a woman she'd known for most of her life. A woman who apparently counted on inheriting Dr. Nance's house and a great deal of cash from his estate.

Keeping a sharp lookout, she pulled out the paperwork. The first document was Dessie's will. The second was a copy of a marriage license issued ten days ago to Desiree Elizabeth Dupre and Cletus William Darnell. A photograph of a beaming Dessie and Clete had been clipped to the license, along with a Post-it note that read, "Happiest day of my life, babe."

Dessie and Clete were married?

Holy sh—

Nikki went back to the will and quickly thumbed through the pages, noting the beneficiaries that included her sister and two nephews. However, the bulk of Dessie's estate—which would include any inheritance from Dr. Nance—was to be awarded to her husband, Cletus William Darnell, upon her death.

ADAM CAUGHT A blur out of the corner of his eye a split second before he heard the dogs. They sprang from the corner of the building so quickly he barely had time to identify the threat before he turned and sprinted for the fence. Vaulting over, he landed with a hard thud that caused him to stumble. The dogs pressed against the fence, snarling so ferociously he thought they might rip right through the metal links.

He started to make a run for the woods, then hit the dirt as a bullet whizzed over his head. Another skimmed the air not five feet from where he lay. He pivoted his head, keeping his cheek pressed to the ground as he pinpointed the shooter. The man had climbed to the top of one of the crushed car stacks after letting the dogs out. When he saw that he had Adam's attention, he lifted the rifle and fired off another round, the crack echoing down through the metal canyons. Evidently, *Trespassers Will Be Shot* was more than an idle threat, although from his vantage, even a mediocre marksman could have hit his target.

Which was why Adam didn't pull his weapon and return fire. The thought had occurred to him that the man's intent might be to provoke a gunfight so that taking out an armed and dangerous intruder on his property would be justified. Shooting a fleeing trespasser—a cop, no less—in broad daylight would likely get the man locked up, even in Texas.

While he reloaded, Adam leaped to his feet and dashed for cover, allowing the shadows at the tree line to swallow him up before he dared to glance back. The dogs had disappeared, but the man with the rifle retained his position on top of the crushed cars. Another thought came to Adam a split second before he bolted into the woods. What if the man's real objective was to drive him into the swamp, where disposing of a body would be easier?

Despite that possibility, he kept going, zigzagging through the brush and trees until he finally had to stop to get his bearings. He'd run in the opposite direction of the road. At some point, he needed to double back and find his vehicle. Not yet, though. Not until he'd put a little more breathing room between him and that rifle.

He didn't hear any sounds of pursuit. Not at first. He slowed to a comfortable stride. A breeze sifted through the pine trees, bringing the scent of the swamp. The ground grew soft beneath his feet as the canopy overhead thickened. Spanish moss dripped down from the branches, swaying like tangled hair in the wind.

Adam slowed yet again as he approached a murky channel that undoubtedly fed into the lake at some point. Lily pads carpeted the water, reminding him of the spot where he'd found Dr. Nance's body. He didn't see a corpse now, only the sinewy glide of a water moccasin, its dark, thick head lifted on a slender neck as it skimmed across the surface. As he watched, another snake slid from the bank into the water and yet a third slithered along the top of a partially submerged log.

He started to turn away from the infested water when a sound came to him through the trees, distant but headed his way. The dogs had been turned loose in the woods.

Another rifle blast startled a heron from the shallow water. Rather than directly behind him, the shot had come from his right. The man was on the road now, herding him away from his vehicle.

Adam glanced around. He might have been able to scurry up a tree to avoid the dogs or even camouflage his scent with mud, if he dared get that close to the snaky water. But a human predator wouldn't be so easily fooled or discouraged. Maybe he was letting his imagination get the better of him, but Adam had the uncanny notion that he wasn't the hunter's first two-legged prey.

Turning, he sprinted through the trees, trying to outpace his pursuer while retaining a vague sense of direction in his head. The channel should run out to the highway, where it would connect with the lake underneath one of the bridges, but he'd overshoot his vehicle if he went that far. He needed to cut back to his right.

The dogs were closing in. He could hear them tearing through the underbrush behind him. A car engine sounded nearby. He was closer to the road than he realized. All he had to do was get to the tree line and find his vehicle.

The car skidded to a halt and a door slammed. Adam could hear muted voices through the trees, and for a moment, he thought about calling out to the newcomer. Surely, the shooter's trigger finger would be a little less itchy in front of a witness. Adam held his position and listened. The woods seemed uncannily silent. Was it over now that a point had been made?

He wanted to believe the guy had given up and was headed back home with his dogs, but no such luck. A shouted command caused the canines to yelp in excitement. A car door slammed again. Adam could hear the low rev of the engine as the vehicle crept along the road, patrolling the edge of the woods.

Had someone else joined in the chase? If so, what was his next move? He was still on private property and that put him in a precarious legal position. He had no shield, no standing, and he was a long way from his jurisdiction. He doubted an unofficial arrangement with the coroner's office would carry much weight.

So far, the man had only fired warning shots. Adam had to be careful here. Not only his career, but also the rest of his life could be at stake. The best thing he could do was to avoid confrontation. He had no choice but to turn back and follow the channel all the way out to the highway. He'd arrange to pick up his vehicle at a later time.

The dogs were closing in again. By the time he reached the sloping bank, they were nearly on him. They came at him fast. He didn't have time to draw his weapon. He barely had time to throw up an arm to fend off the first attack. He tried to brace for impact, but he lost his footing and tumbled down the muddy incline to the water's edge.

The dogs stood rigid at the top of the grade, hackles lifted along their sleek backs. Adam sprang to his feet and plunged into the stagnant water, trying not to think about the moccasins as he waded out chest-deep and dived.

He didn't know if the dogs had followed him. He sank to the muddy bottom and waited as long as his lungs would allow. When he finally surfaced, he gulped air as he blinked water from his eyes. Once he had his breath, he swept his gaze over the surface of the channel and then upward to the embankment, where the dogs sat quietly at their master's feet.

The man lifted the rifle to his shoulder, took aim over the water and pulled the trigger.

Chapter Twelve

Nikki was seated at the window, staring out at the pool, when Dessie came back into the kitchen several minutes later. She'd thought about slipping outside to call Adam, but she didn't want to arouse Dessie's suspicions. She settled for sending him a quick text, along with the photographs she'd snapped of the will and marriage license. Her thumbs hovered over the keypad as she waited for a response. When none was forthcoming, she slid the phone back into her bag and turned with a strained smile.

"Everything okay?" she asked Dessie.

"Yes. Sorry it took so long, but you know how Lila Wilkes is when she gets wound up. She doesn't know how to take a hint."

"It's okay. I was just texting a friend." Nikki nodded to the covered dish in Dessie's hands. "She really did bring over another casserole."

"Blackberry cobbler this time. Still warm from the oven." Dessie removed the top and drew in the aroma. "Say what you will about the woman, but she knows her way around a kitchen."

Questions swirled in Nikki's head as she kept right on smiling.

Ask her about the marriage license. Ask her about the will. Tell her what you overheard the night before and see how she reacts.

Not yet, she decided. Better to play this out for a little while longer and see if Dessie let something slip.

Her hands were still trembling, Nikki realized. She clasped her fingers together in her lap. "That was Lila at the door? Did she come to badger you again about the funeral service?"

Dessie cocked her head in confusion. "Did I mention she'd been here before about the funeral?"

Too late, Nikki remembered she wasn't supposed to know about Lila's previous visits. The contents of that envelope had left her rattled and now she was the one who had let something slip. "She came by my house after work on Friday," Nikki said with a shrug. "I assumed she'd been by here as well."

"Three times already. She doesn't know when to give up."

"She is persistent," Nikki agreed.

"Even so, it'd be a shame to let a perfectly good cobbler go to waste," Dessie said. "Especially when I've got homemade vanilla ice cream in the freezer."

Nikki's first inclination was to decline. After seeing those documents, the last thing she wanted to do was sit at Dr. Nance's breakfast table and make small talk with the woman who apparently stood to gain the most from his death. But she'd come over here to gather information and this was as opportune a time as she'd likely get to be alone with Dessie.

Just be casual. Pretend you never saw that marriage license. Pretend you don't know that Dessie is planning a romantic Caribbean honeymoon with Dr. Nance's attorney.

She summoned another smile. "That would be a shame. I'd love to dig into that cobbler, but only if you're having some, too. And only if you'll let me help."

"You can get the ice cream from the freezer." She returned Nikki's smile. "It'll be just like old times."

Nikki dug out the tub of ice cream while Dessie dished up the cobbler. Then they carried their desserts back to the table and sat across from one another.

Nikki sampled the warm blackberries while keeping an eye on her companion. "Yum. You're right. Lila is a good cook. Not as good as you, though."

"Don't let her hear you say that," Dessie warned. "You know Lila. She has to be best at everything, be it growing roses or baking cobblers."

"Or planning funerals."

"That, too."

Nikki let the ice cream melt for a moment. "Did you tell her there wasn't going to be a formal service?"

"I did."

"How did she take it?"

"About as well as you'd expect. Luckily, Clete…Mr. Darnell was there to back me up."

"Yes, that was lucky."

Dessie glanced across the table as if detecting something troubling in Nikki's tone. A frown flickered before she shrugged it away. "Not that it'll make that much difference to Lila. She'll do as she pleases regardless of anyone else's wishes. She always has. She muttered something about a memorial service before she finally left."

"Maybe a memorial service wouldn't be a bad idea," Nikki said. "Just something simple where people in the community can get together to celebrate Dr. Nance's life."

Dessie gave her an odd look. "Nothing is simple once Lila Wilkes gets involved. She turns everything into a production. She loves to be the center of attention, even at someone else's memorial service."

"You don't like her much, do you?" Nikki asked carefully.

Dessie hesitated. "No, I guess I don't. Just between you and me, we've had our problems in the past."

"What kind of problems?"

Dessie looked discomfited. "I shouldn't speak ill of the woman. Especially on a Sunday."

"It's just me," Nikki coaxed.

Dessie dabbed her lips. "Don't get me wrong. She's done a lot of good things in this town. Been a real blessing to the elderly. I don't know what some folks around here would do without her. But she's always had a problem with boundaries."

"What do you mean?"

"She used to think nothing of calling Dr. Nance in the middle of the night or showing up here at all hours to ask about a medication or treatment for someone she was looking after. Half the time, he wasn't even the person's doctor. I finally had to tell her she needed to respect his personal time. Either go to the ER or make an appointment."

"What did she say to that?"

"She didn't like it, but that wasn't the first time I'd had to call her out. We had some of the same issues when she first came to town."

Nikki idly stirred the melted ice cream into the gooey filling. "She told me a little about her move here. She said Dr. Nance was the one who tracked her down and convinced her to come to Belle Pointe to care for her aunt."

Dessie's mouth thinned. "He tracked her down. I don't know how much convincing he had to do."

"Yes, I got the impression she hadn't exactly resisted the idea." Nikki glanced up. "You were already working for Dr. Nance at the time?"

Dessie nodded. "I started here right after his wife died. Part-time at first until I moved into the garage apartment. Then I took on more responsibilities. Not just cooking and cleaning, but paying bills, overseeing repairs, that sort of thing. My mama raised me to be plainspoken, so maybe I wasn't as tactful as I should have been with someone like Lila. She's…needy. But Dr. Nance had suffered a terrible tragedy and he was working himself to death just trying to cope with the loss. I felt very protective of him."

"What did Lila do?"

"Besides the phone calls and the unannounced visits? Sometimes she'd go to the hospital to try and catch him between rounds. I guess she thought since he was the one who brought her here, she was entitled to his undivided time and attention. I stepped in and put a stop to it then, and later when things got out of hand again."

Dessie's candor surprised Nikki, even though she'd come here looking for answers. She'd gotten an eyeful snooping into that envelope and now she was getting an earful about Lila Wilkes. But a strange sense of unease dampened her excitement. The thought occurred to her that maybe Dessie was playing her, revealing information calculated to distract and mislead.

Nikki put that thought aside and tried to maintain a neutral tone. "Do you think Lila had romantic feelings for Dr. Nance?"

Dessie seemed to consider the question carefully. "I have wondered about that at times. It would explain a lot." Her gaze sharpened. "Why? Did she say something to you?"

"Only that she had a crush on him when she first came here. She said everyone in town did."

Dessie scowled. "I don't know about everyone, but I reckon he was considered a catch. A young, handsome widower and a doctor, to boot. He could have had his pick of lady friends, and I doubt Lila Wilkes would have been high on that list."

Nikki thought about Tom Brannon's suggestion that something may have gone on between Dessie and Dr. Nance. Was that the reason Dessie had felt so protective of him? The real reason for her animosity toward Lila Wilkes?

"This may sound strange, but did Lila ever stalk Dr. Nance? You said she used to turn up at the hospital to see him. That's pretty aggressive behavior."

"Well, that's Lila. She's a bulldozer when she wants something."

"Did you ever catch her snooping through his things?"

The question seemed to catch Dessie off guard. "Snooping through his things? What are you talking about?"

"At some point in time, someone came into this house and took Dr. Nance's gold watch from the mantel in his study. Instead of selling such an expensive timepiece, the thief hid it under a floorboard at the Ruins. Maybe I'm reaching, but that seems personal to me. That watch meant a lot to him."

Dessie's gaze widened. "You think Lila Wilkes took his watch?"

"Maybe she thought she could somehow sever his ties to his dead wife. Or if she felt rejected, maybe she was trying to hurt him. Who knows? That kind of behavior isn't rational. Did she have access to the house?"

"You mean did she have a key? Not that I know of, but she wouldn't have needed one to get in. Dr. Nance was always careless about locking up. I was forever finding doors and windows open. Anyone could have come in at almost any time."

"Did anything besides the gold watch ever go missing?"

"No, but..." Dessie trailed off.

Nikki leaned in anxiously. "What?"

"It's probably nothing. Just my own absentmindedness. About the time when we first realized the watch had been stolen, I noticed things in other parts of the house had been moved around. Like someone had purposefully gone from room to room rearranging his belongings."

"Did you tell Dr. Nance?"

"Yes, and for a while, he was a little better at locking up, especially at night, but when nothing else happened, he eventually fell back into his old ways." Her gaze lifted. "Why are you asking all these questions, Nikki? Is there something you're not telling me?"

"I'm just trying to gather information."

Dessie wasn't buying it. "What kind of information?"

"Anything that will help to establish the cause, manner and circumstances of Dr. Nance's death."

Dessie blinked in confusion. "But Sheriff Brannon came to the house and told me in this very kitchen that Dr. Nance had drowned in Echo Lake. He said they found his fishing boat down by the bridge."

"That's true," Nikki said. "However, I'm not yet convinced the drowning was accidental."

The spoon slipped from Dessie's fingers and clattered against the bowl. She wiped frantically at the splatters with her napkin. "What are you saying? You can't think someone…" She closed her eyes briefly and drew a quick breath. "I can't bring myself to even think such a thing, let alone say it."

Nikki gave her a sympathetic nod. "I know. I feel the same way. It's a terrible thing to contemplate. That someone he knew and trusted…someone *we* know… could have deliberately harmed him."

Dessie said a little desperately, "You're the coroner. A pathologist. Can't you tell about such things?"

"Not always. Not after that long in the water. The body starts to break down—"

"Don't!" Dessie looked horrified. "Please. I don't want to have that image in my head."

"I'm sorry." Nikki reached across the table and

squeezed her hand. "I don't mean to upset you. Maybe his death was an accident. Maybe he took the boat out in the dark, got confused on the water and rammed into the bridge pilings. But that's a lot of maybes and there are still too many unanswered questions. Do you have any idea why he changed his mind at the last minute about his trip to Houston?"

"No. I was as surprised as anyone to learn that he'd gone to the lake instead."

"Did you worry when you didn't hear from him?"

"He rarely called when he was away," Dessie said. "I didn't think anything of it until Sheriff Brannon showed up at the door."

"You were here the whole time he was gone? You couldn't have missed a call?"

"Not the *whole* time. I had errands to run, groceries to buy, normal, everyday duties to attend to."

"I meant you were in town," Nikki clarified. "You didn't take a trip or anything." *Or go on a quickie honeymoon?*

Dessie hesitated. "Where do you think I would have gone to?"

"Nowhere. I don't think anything. I'm just asking questions."

"Yes, and a lot of them."

"I'm sorry. I'm just trying to do my job, that's all. I want to do right by Dr. Nance."

Dessie shook her head forlornly. "You really think someone could have killed him?"

"I think it's possible."

She stared at Nikki for the longest time. Something gleamed in the depths of her eyes, but Nikki couldn't place the emotion. Fear? Guilt? If she had to guess, the dark glint seemed more like anger. "Who do you think did it?"

"I don't know yet. As I said, I'm still trying to gather information. It sounds crazy to even ask this, but did he have any enemies?"

"Enemies?" She looked appalled. "Everyone loved the man."

"What about arguments or disagreements, even something that seemed trivial at the time? Anything at all come to mind?"

Dessie's expression seemed to harden. "You know as well as I do that Dr. Nance got along with everyone. He could charm the birds out of the trees when he set his mind to it."

"What about at the clinic or hospital?"

"I'm sure there were differences of opinion from time to time. He was never shy about speaking his mind. But people respected him for that."

"What about Dr. Wingate?" Nikki asked. "Any problems with the partnership?"

Dessie's gaze turned shrewd. "Why? What did you hear?"

"I didn't hear anything," Nikki said. "But I saw Dr. Wingate at Dr. Nance's cabin last night."

"Last night? What was she doing there?" Dessie's tone shifted. "What were you doing there?"

"I went out to the lake to visit a friend and we saw a light in the cabin. We thought someone might have broken in. Apparently, Dr. Wingate let herself in with a key that Dr. Nance gave her a long time ago. She seemed concerned that he'd removed some medical records from the clinic before he died. She said the cabin was the last place she could think to look for them. Did she or anyone else from the clinic come to the house to search his study?"

"Not while I've been here." Dessie didn't look at all pleased that a casual conversation had turned into an interrogation. Nikki could hardly blame her. "I haven't heard from Dr. Wingate since we found out about Dr. Nance. Not one word."

"As I said, she had a key to the cabin. Is there any reason she would have a key to this house? Maybe she came while you were out."

"I don't think so, but like I said, if someone wanted in badly enough, they could have found a way."

Yes, Nikki could attest to that. She cleared her throat. "Dr. Nance apparently told his assistant that he needed the files for some mysterious project he was working on. You told Sheriff Brannon he'd been coming home from the clinic and shutting himself up in his study. When you asked, he said he was working on a puzzle. Do you think those files could be related?"

Dessie shrugged. "I wouldn't know anything about those files."

"He didn't say anything else about this mysterious puzzle or project? You don't have any idea what he was working on?"

"I cooked and cleaned and stayed out of his business as much as I could. It wasn't my job to ask a lot of questions."

"But the two of you were friends. Maybe he let something slip in everyday conversation. Think back, Dessie. This could be important."

"Nikki, are you saying what I think you're saying?"

"I'm just gathering information, remember?"

"About Dr. Wingate?"

"About anyone connected to Dr. Nance."

"I guess you'll be asking questions about me next." She gave Nikki a peculiar look. "Maybe you already have."

Oh, I have questions for you, Dessie. You've no idea. How long have you been seeing Clete Darnell romantically? Whose idea was it to get married so quickly and then change your will? Why keep the union a secret if everything is on the up-and-up? "Right now we're talking about Dr. Wingate."

Dessie's gaze seemed knowing, but maybe that was Nikki's imagination.

She took another stab. "I can't help thinking that Dr. Wingate is going to a lot of trouble to find those files. She claimed she's worried about patient privacy, but I'm not so sure." Nikki paused. "Did you know that Dr. Nance was planning to retire when he came back from Houston?"

Dessie's brows shot up. "*Retire?* Who told you that?"

"Dr. Wingate said he'd been having some issues at the clinic."

"What issues?"

"According to her, he'd been forgetting appointments and mixing up prescriptions. Things had gotten to the point where she felt she had to step in. Dr. Nance agreed to phase out his practice when he returned from his trip."

Dessie folded her arms. "I don't believe a word of

it. He would have said something if he was planning to leave the clinic."

"But you told Sheriff Brannon that you'd also noticed a change in his behavior."

"Yes. He was distant and distracted. At times, he seemed to have the weight of the world on his shoulders. But I never said anything about memory issues." She grew pensive. "Now you've got me to wondering about Dr. Wingate. You think there's something incriminating about her in those files?"

"That's what I'd like to find out."

"She said he'd been forgetting things, did she? Well, that's convenient. If he was on to her, maybe she was trying to make him look unreliable. What better way to clear herself than by casting doubt on Dr. Nance?"

"You think she made up the incidents at the clinic?"

"Maybe not altogether. We all forget things as we get older. I know I do. But she could have exaggerated what happened." Dessie gave Nikki a long look. "You know how that works. Plant the seed of doubt and people will start looking for mistakes."

"That would be a pretty devious and sophisticated maneuver."

"Sounds about right." Dessie's gaze never wavered. "I've known Dr. Wingate for a long time. She's nothing if not clever."

So Dessie also had a problem with Patience Wingate. Nikki was beginning to think she'd never known the real Dessie Dupre at all. She'd always thought of her as a modest and unassuming woman. Not a mouse by any means, but someone who led a quiet life and did her best to get along. Evidently, neither the real Dessie

Dupre nor the real Dr. Nance matched the descriptions Nikki had carried with her all these years.

People were complicated, even the quiet ones. Especially the quiet ones. Look at her.

She leaned in. "Dessie, what do you know about Dr. Wingate that I don't?"

The woman spoke without hesitation, as if she were suddenly relieved that someone had allowed her to open the floodgates. "You know I'm not one to talk out of school, but it's always been my job to look after Dr. Nance. I see no reason to stop now."

"Go on."

"He and Dr. Wingate had an affair. It ended badly."

"An affair?" Nikki wondered how she could still be surprised after all the afternoon's revelations.

Dessie nodded. "She had a family. When her husband found out about Dr. Nance, he left and took their kids with him. Things got ugly. The divorce and custody battle cost her a fortune. When her relationship with Dr. Nance didn't work out, she blamed him for ruining her life. It got so bad that Dr. Nance offered to buy out her partnership. She refused to sell, partly out of spite, but mostly because she wouldn't have had much of a practice without his referrals and everyone knew it. Eventually, they worked things out, but it took a long time."

Nikki shook her head. "How did I not hear about this? It must have caused a scandal, but I never heard a word."

"You were away at school at the time. You didn't come home much those first few years. Despite the ugliness, they managed to keep things quiet. Only a few people knew."

"I can't imagine keeping something like that quiet in a town like Belle Pointe."

"You'd be surprised at all the secrets." Dessie paused to stare out the window as she gathered her thoughts. "If you're looking for a reason for someone to take that watch, maybe you should talk to Dr. Wingate. In her eyes, Dr. Nance took everything from her. Maybe she decided to take the one thing that meant the most to him."

"JUST TAKE IT EASY," Adam called across the water as he slowly got to his feet.

The man returned his stare through the riflescope. "Hands in the air! Nice and slow-like. Atta boy."

Arms lifted, Adam backed toward the opposite bank. The mud sucked at his shoes, limiting his mobility and, therefore, any desperate attempt at escape. He could draw his weapon, but where would that get him? Facedown in the swamp, most likely.

He squinted into the sun. "I'm a cop. My name is Adam Thayer. I'm a homicide detective with the Dallas Police Department."

"You think I don't already know that? Nobody enters this county without me knowing about it."

Adam kept his hands lifted while he surveyed his surroundings. "I don't want any trouble."

"You should have thought about that earlier. I don't think you appreciate the seriousness of your offense. Around here, we don't care much for trespassers and snoops. As a matter of fact, we don't care much for cops, either."

"Let me walk out of here and this ends now," Adam said. "No one has to get hurt."

"I'll decide when and how this ends," the man said. "You better think long and hard about how you answer this question. What's your business in Belle Pointe?"

"I've been temporarily assigned to the Nance County coroner's office. I'm down here investigating a suspicious death."

"The *coroner's* office." The man's head lifted before he reseated the rifle against his shoulder. "You're working for that Dresden woman?"

"Do you know Dr. Dresden? Let me call her. She'll vouch for my credentials."

"You're not calling anyone and your association with Nikki Dresden is reason enough for me to shoot you on the spot. Maybe you're one of them and maybe you're not, but *maybe* it's best not to take any chances."

"I don't know what you're talking about."

"I'm talking about devil-worshippers. Satanists. Call 'em what you want, but the Dresden woman was their ringleader back in the day. She was the one who called all the shots. Maybe she still does, for all anyone knows."

"Those old rumors were unfounded," Adam said. "Surely you know that."

The man's head lifted. "Unfounded by who? Not by me. Not by anyone else I know. Ask around and you'll get an earful. Fifteen years ago, she and her little Goth friends killed a girl. Lured her to the Ruins, cut out her heart for one of their black rituals and then buried her body where it won't ever be found."

Adam couldn't tell if the guy was putting him on or not. No one in their right mind could still believe any of that stuff. But he had a sudden inkling of what Nikki must have had to put up with all these years.

He countered the man's assertion with a logical query. "If they buried her body where it'll never be found, how do you know what they did to her?"

"It's called common sense. Everybody knows what they did." He gestured with the barrel of the rifle. "Enough small talk. You told me why you came to Belle Pointe. Now tell me what you're doing on my property."

"I'd like to ask you some questions."

"If you want to ask someone a question, you get him on the phone. You don't go prowling around a man's private domain unless you have a death wish. Or unless you're just plain stupid. I'd be within my rights to put a bullet through your chest. Although I've always been partial to headshots."

"You can't shoot someone in broad daylight for trespassing and expect to get away with it," Adam said. "You'd have a hard time proving deadly threat with me out here unarmed and you up there with a rifle."

"Since when does a cop walk around unarmed?"

The man lowered the rifle. "Besides, I don't have to shoot you. I can just sic the dogs on you. Right, boys?"

One of the dogs got up and came to the edge of the embankment to growl a warning. Adam stood frozen with his hands in the air.

"Or we could just leave you out here and let the gators and moccasins nibble on you."

"A cop disappears, people are going to come looking for him," Adam said.

"They can look all they want, but a body doesn't last long in the swamp." He cocked his head. "Ever been bit by a cottonmouth? My cousin was once. Damn thing crawled in his boat. He said the strike felt like someone had whacked him on the knee with a red-hot poker. Nearly lost his leg and he got to the doctor real quick. Imagine if you had to walk out of here. Probably wouldn't make it to the highway. That's what happens when you go poking your nose in places it doesn't belong."

"Like Dr. Nance's cabin? That was you the other night, wasn't it?" Adam was getting tired of the man's threats. *Put up or shut up.* "What were you doing snooping around someone else's private property?"

"You're asking the wrong question, buddy. Maybe you should have stayed back in Dallas, where you belong."

Adam scouted the terrain from his periphery. No way he could make a run for it. He was still too far away from either bank. He tried to calculate the odds of drawing his weapon and getting off a shot before the man took him out with the rifle. Slim to none, he decided.

"You let me walk out of here right now and that's the end of it," Adam said. "You haven't broken any laws yet. At least none that will get you arrested. Even if I tell this story to the sheriff, he'll likely pat you on the back for your restraint."

"Tell you what I'll do." The man hunkered down between the dogs. "I'll give you a head start. You make it to the opposite bank by the time I count to twenty and I'll give you another twenty count to get to the woods. After that, all bets are off."

"Or I could just shoot you," Adam said.

"Yeah, I figured you were packing. You go for that weapon, you best be quick. Otherwise, time to turn tail and run." He lifted the rifle. "One Mississippi… two Mississippi…"

Chapter Thirteen

Late that afternoon, Nikki sat on her back steps, watching the sun sink below the treetops. Despite the deep quiet of her garden, she couldn't relax. She knew too much now. Her visit to Dessie had opened a Pandora's box, but rather than answering all those lingering questions, the revelations had only deepened her suspicions. Everyone had secrets, it seemed. She was no exception. She suspected Adam wasn't, either.

Where was he? She hadn't heard from him all day. When she came home earlier from her visit with Dessie, she'd tried to reach him, but the call went straight to voice mail. She'd left a message, asking that he get in touch with her immediately. They needed to talk about the photographs she'd texted him earlier. She didn't want to explain her discoveries over the phone. They needed to speak in person.

An hour went by and then two. The sun slid beneath the horizon and the breeze picked up. She left another message and then considered driving out to the lake. Maybe he was just busy. Or maybe he had company. Maybe he'd packed his bags in the middle of the night and gone back to Dallas.

And maybe you're being ridiculous.

But she couldn't shake the notion that something was wrong. Uneasiness prickled her nape as she peered into the deepening shadows. *Where are you?*

He'd said he would call today. Why hadn't he?

She picked up her phone and sent another text. Still no response.

Rising from the steps, she started to go inside and grab her bag when she heard a car pull into her driveway. She ran down the steps and cut through the back gate just as Adam was climbing out of his SUV. Even in the fading light, she could see that his windshield was shattered and the hood crumpled down the middle as if someone had struck it with a baseball bat. She rushed forward, resisting the urge to fling herself in his arms.

"What happened?" she said on a breath. "Were you in an accident? Are you okay?"

"I'm fine. Can't say the same for my vehicle."

She took another survey of the damage. "How did that happen?"

"A tire iron would be my guess."

She caught her breath. "When? Where?"

"I got caught someplace I shouldn't have been. When I finally made it back to my vehicle, the damage had been done."

"That's cryptic." Nikki took a moment to calm her racing pulse. "Did you file a police report?"

"Not yet. I wanted to touch base with you first, make sure you're okay."

"I'm fine," she said anxiously. "But I knew something was wrong. I've left messages for you all afternoon. When you didn't return my calls or texts, I worried that something had happened."

His expression gentled in the soft light. "I'm sorry. I didn't mean to worry you. My phone got wet and my grandmother's house no longer has a working land-line." He turned so that the light hit him just right, re-vealing a fresh scratch across his cheek.

Nikki said in alarm, "Adam, what happened to your face?"

He put a hand to his cheek. "It's just a scratch. It looks worse than it is. I don't even know when it hap-pened. Probably scraped it against a tree branch when I ran from the dogs."

"What?"

He gave her a look. "It's been an eventful after-noon."

"And I thought I had news. If your phone was ru-ined, you didn't see the photographs I texted you." She took his chin in her fingers and turned his face to the light to inspect the fresh damage. "Let's go inside. I'll put something on it."

He pulled back slightly. "It'll keep. What photo-graphs?"

"I'll tell you inside. No sense courting infection."

"Nikki—"

"First things first," she insisted. "We'll take care of that scratch and then get you something to eat. Are you hungry? We could order takeout."

"Maybe later. I had a quick bite when I went back to the house to shower and change. I didn't want to come over here smelling like the swamp."

"You have had an afternoon."

"Sounds like we both have. I don't need anything to eat, but I could sure use a drink. Something stronger than tea if you have it."

"I'll see what I can find. Adam?" She started for the house, then paused and said over her shoulder, "Trouble really does seem to follow you, doesn't it?"

"I guess you could argue that I sometimes go out looking for it." He turned to scan the street. "Dark things are happening in this town, Nikki. Dr. Nance was right about that. He really was on to something. I think whatever he found out may have something to do with Dr. Wingate and the man who owns a salvage yard ten miles outside of town."

"Eddie Bowman?" Her eyes widened. "Did he do that to your car? You were running from *his* dogs?"

"Apparently he doesn't take kindly to trespassers."

"You shouldn't have gone out there alone," she scolded. "Why did you go out there in the first place? And why didn't you tell me what you had in mind? I would have warned you about Bowman."

"No time. I followed Dr. Wingate out there."

"You what?" Nikki's agitation accelerated. "Why were you tailing Dr. Wingate?"

"I told you last night I had a hunch she was hiding something. Somehow this Eddie Bowman is involved."

"Eddie Bowman is a thug. From what I hear, he deals a lot more than used car parts out of that junkyard."

"Drugs?"

"Drugs, guns, you name it."

Adam nodded thoughtfully. "That would explain some things."

"I'm serious, Adam. You need to be careful with that guy. Everyone in town knows he's bad news."

"I've dealt with plenty of guys like Eddie Bowman in my time."

Twilight had deepened, but Nikki could still see the gleam in his eyes and the curve of his lips as he stared down at her. Without warning, he reached over and tucked an errant strand of hair behind her ear. "I appreciate your concern, though."

Nikki closed her eyes at his touch. Something was happening here. She could live in denial all she wanted, but the quivers in her stomach and the pounding of her pulse didn't lie. "Come inside," she said on a shiver. "I'll tell you about those photographs."

ADAM SAT ON the edge of the bathtub while Nikki swabbed the scratch. Minutes earlier, she'd dug a bottle of whiskey out of a kitchen cabinet and poured him a generous shot. He'd downed the contents in one swallow, leaving the empty glass on the counter as he followed her into the bathroom. He hadn't had a drink in months and the eighty-proof alcohol packed a punch. He savored the slow burn at the back of his throat and the warmth in the pit of his stomach.

He enjoyed Nikki's nearness, too, especially when she leaned into him. He smelled roses, but he couldn't tell if the scent came from her skin or her hair or from the bushes that cascaded over her back fence. Her touch was soft and deft. She finished with the antiseptic and turned to put everything away.

She talked while she worked, giving him a detailed debriefing of her visit with Dessie Dupre. When she came to the part about the marriage license and will, he whistled softly. "Clete Darnell doesn't fool around, does he? He takes over the practice in May, persuades Dr. Nance to update his will and then moves in on Dessie, marries her and rewrites *her* will all in the space of what—three months?"

"If that." Nikki washed her hands at the sink and reached for a towel. "I've been thinking about the conversation I overheard in the study last night. They were obviously looking for something. What if Dr. Nance never updated his will? What if Clete Darnell drew up a new will leaving everything to Dessie and then forged Dr. Nance's signature? Taking over the previous attorney's practice gave him the opportunity to destroy the original will, but he'd need to make certain there weren't any copies lying around in case someone decided to contest Dessie's inheritance."

"You've known Dessie for a long time. You think she's capable of that kind of deception, let alone murder?"

Nikki frowned. "I don't want to. I desperately want to believe she's the person I've always thought her to be. But the Dessie I knew wouldn't have been conned by someone like Clete Darnell. The kind and conscientious woman who always took such good care of Dr. Nance wouldn't be planning a trip to the Caribbean just days after his body was found floating in the lake. I'm beginning to think that no one in this town is who they claim to be."

"We all have a dark side," Adam said. "The evil twin that rides on our shoulder and whispers bad things in our ear."

"That's a pleasant thought." She hung up the towel and turned to the bathroom door. "Come on. Let's go sit outside now that it's cooled off. I could use some fresh air."

"Be right there. Just give me a minute to grab the whiskey."

He got down another glass from the cabinet and carried everything outside.

"It's cooler tonight," he said. "Nice change from the sweltering heat."

Nikki drew up her knees and wrapped her arms around her legs. "I don't know why but the end of summer always makes me nostalgic."

"For what?"

"That's the thing. I don't know. I certainly don't long for my childhood, much less my high school years."

"No one longs for high school." He sat down beside her on the steps and poured the whiskey.

She turned to face him. "Unless you're one of the golden people."

"The what?"

"You know. The chosen ones. The in crowd. The same group of popular kids who runs every high school. People like you, I imagine."

He sat back, propping his elbows on the step above him. "What makes you think I was popular in high school?"

"I could tell the moment I laid eyes on you. You have a certain look. All that oozing confidence. We misfits can always pick you out of a crowd."

"Is that so?"

"Yeah." She lifted her drink, their gazes meeting over the rim of the glass. She glanced away.

"Sounds a little judgmental to me," he said.

"I'm not judging. Just making an observation."

But there was an edge in her tone. Things were getting a little too personal. She was creating distance. Putting all those walls back up. Adam sipped his drink and watched the flutter of expressions across her face.

"You still haven't told me what happened to you today," she said. "How did you get crossways with Eddie Bowman?"

He allowed her to change the subject without comment. "Let's just say it involved a rifle, two German shepherds and a swamp full of pit vipers."

Her eyes widened. "I'm impressed you lived to tell the tale."

"Do you have any idea why Dr. Wingate would be mixed up with a guy like Bowman?"

Nikki shrugged. "Not really. But Dessie told me that Dr. Wingate and Dr. Nance had an affair some years back. She was married at the time. The divorce got messy and expensive, and when her relationship with Dr. Nance ended, she blamed him for everything."

"But they continued to work together?" Adam grimaced. "That must have been awkward." His ex worked in the DA's office and even that was too close for comfort.

"Dessie said he tried to buy her out but she wouldn't sell. The clinic has always been a gold mine and I guess she needed the money after a lengthy custody battle."

"And Bowman?"

"This is just a guess, but after I left Dessie earlier,

I started thinking about one of the first death scenes I attended as coroner. It was an OD. The deceased's wife told me that he'd been able to get his hands on an endless supply of drugs, opioids mostly, because he knew a guy who had a deal with a doctor."

"The guy was Eddie Bowman?"

"She called him the junkman. I thought junk as in drugs. It never occurred to me at the time that she was referring to Bowman or that the doctor in question might have been Dr. Wingate. But it makes sense if the divorce wiped her out financially. She doesn't strike me as the type who could get along on a budget. And she certainly doesn't appear to be hurting for money now. It would also explain why she's so anxious to get her hands on those files. Maybe Dr. Nance found something that could incriminate her."

"It would also explain a few other things," Adam said. "She and Bowman were arguing when I saw them together this afternoon. She threw an envelope at him. I didn't get a look at the contents, but I'm guessing it was some kind of payoff."

"Payoff for what, I wonder."

"That's the question. Blackmail, maybe. Or something more insidious like murder for hire, if this guy is as bad as you say he is."

"You think she hired Bowman to kill Dr. Nance?"

"It's a theory. A big guy like that wouldn't have any trouble manhandling Dr. Nance into his boat, especially if he'd been drugged."

"We have no proof of any of this," Nikki said.

"Not yet we don't," Adam agreed. "The thing is, he claimed to know that I'm a cop. He said no one moves

into this town without him knowing about it. He could
have just been blowing smoke, but it makes you wonder. Maybe someone found out that Dr. Nance con-
tacted me and asked me to come down here to look
into things. Maybe that same someone told Bowman
to be on the lookout for me."

"Dr. Wingate?"

"It would have been easy enough for her to eaves-
drop on a phone call. I'd really like to get a look inside Bowman's office. See if I can find out what was
in that envelope. If there's anything tying him to Dr.
Wingate, that's where the evidence will be."

Nikki searched his features in the dark. "You're not
seriously considering going out there alone, I hope. I'll
say it again. Eddie Bowman isn't someone you want to
tangle with. He's been trouble for as long as I can remember. He used to do handyman work around town.
He could fix anything. People said he was the best car-
penter in Nance County, but my grandmother would
never allow him in her house. Like I said, she wasn't
a kind woman, but she was a good judge of character."

"She sounds like an interesting woman," Adam
said.

"Interesting?" Nikki grew pensive. "Yes, I suppose
she was."

"You didn't get along?"

"We didn't *not* get along. We pretty much kept out
of each other's way. But that wasn't her fault. She got
saddled with me when my parents skipped town. First
my dad and then my mom."

"Are they still alive?"

"I have no idea." She stirred restlessly. "I don't want

to talk about them. I want to hear more about Eddie Bowman and your theory."

Adam figured Eddie Bowman was pretty far down on her list of appealing topics, but anything to keep him at arm's distance.

"Do you think he was the guy at Dr. Nance's cabin the other night?" she asked.

"That's a fair bet," Adam said with a nod.

"And yet you want to go back out to the salvage yard and snoop around some more." She gave him an accusing look. "You know what I think? I think you like living on the edge. Not me. I like things quiet."

He shot her an amused glance. "I don't know if I buy that. Taking those photographs this afternoon was pretty damn risky. But I agree that quiet can sometimes be nice." He gestured toward her backyard. "It's certainly peaceful out here. And fragrant with all the roses. You've a green thumb, apparently."

"Hardly. I didn't plant any of this. I'm a little surprised I've been able to keep the garden alive. I'm better with dead things."

"Pun intended, I assume." He leaned back on his elbows again. "Why did you choose pathology as a specialty? You didn't want the glory of being a surgeon?"

"I'm like you—I like puzzles. I like looking for clues and signs that everyone else has missed. There's a great deal of satisfaction in finding something that makes all the pieces snap together."

She was passionate about her work. He could hear that in her voice. "And your job as coroner?"

"Oh, I got railroaded into that one. The position was vacant and Tom Brannon saw a sucker. He and

Dr. Nance persuaded a judge to appoint me to the position until a special election could be held. That was nearly two years ago."

Adam said a little too casually, "You and Tom Brannon seem pretty tight."

She frowned. "I wouldn't go that far. We're friends. We work well together. Beyond that…" She shrugged again. "He's a good guy who happens to be engaged to Riley Cavanaugh's sister."

"Small world."

"Small town." She took another sip of her drink. "My turn to ask the questions."

"Fire away."

She gave him a sly look. "You're a cop of a certain age. Early to midthirties, I'd guess. There must be at least one ex-wife in your past."

"It's a myth that the divorce rate among law enforcement personnel is higher than the national average."

"So…no ex-wife?"

"Ex-fiancée," he conceded. "She broke off the engagement a few months ago."

"*She* broke it off? What happened?"

His first inclination was to clam up the way Nikki had about her parents, but then he thought, what the hell? He hadn't talked honestly about the breakup to anyone, even his shrink. Maybe he was due a cathartic heart-to-heart. "The shooting took a toll on our relationship. The surgeries, the long recovery, the months of physical therapy. It was grueling. And Steph has never been the most patient person even in the best of times."

Nikki looked appalled. "She left you because you were injured?"

"Looking back, the breakup had been brewing for a long time. My injuries and the long recovery just brought everything to a head." Funny how he could talk about it now as if it had happened to someone else. He felt an interesting sense of detachment. "The investigation into the shooting got swept under the rug because a politician's kid was involved and powerful people pulled a lot of strings. I didn't like it and said so. Loudly. The powers-that-be decided to delay my reinstatement until I adjusted my attitude. Stephanie caught some flak at the DA's office because of me. I think that's when she decided to end things for good."

Nikki said nothing, but her fierce gaze said a lot. Or was he only imagining the angry glint in her eyes? Maybe he was seeing what he wanted to see. It was gratifying to have someone on his side for a change. Someone he trusted and admired. Someone he might even be falling for a little bit.

"I'm sorry that happened to you," she finally said. "It must have been painful. But sometimes things work out for the best."

He gazed back at her. "Sometimes they do."

The moon was just rising over the treetops. Nikki closed her eyes and tipped her face to the pale light. "I have a confession to make."

"I'm all ears."

"I never said anything, but I remember you now. From that summer, I mean."

"It's about damn time."

She laughed. The sound was light and melodic for such a serious woman.

Right then and there, Adam decided he was going to kiss her. He could just say good-night, get up and leave, and the evening would end pleasantly enough. But she leaned into him. Even placed her hand lightly on his knee. And that was all he needed. The kiss was definitely going to happen.

He relaxed and enjoyed the anticipation. The lightning bugs were out and the crickets. He could smell roses in her hair and honeysuckle from the neighbor's fence.

"You said we first crossed paths at the Ruins, but that's not true," Nikki said. "I first saw you at the lake. You were doing backflips off the bridge."

He nudged her good-naturedly. "Tell the truth. Were you impressed?"

"Very impressed," she said earnestly. "You had long hair back then. And you were very tanned. All lean and sinewy muscles." She caught herself then. "That's the whiskey talking."

He grinned and replenished her glass. "Keep going."

"After that, I saw you at the Ruins. You tried to talk to me once, but—"

"You shut me down."

"I was shy and insecure. I kept my guard up."

"I think that guard is still up," he said.

"Maybe it is, but I'm not the same person I was back then. The girl you saw at the Ruins is gone forever."

"I hope that's not true. She was pretty damn fascinating."

"Most people would say I was just plain weird."

He scoffed. "Most people are afraid of their own damn shadows. They don't know how to react to someone who marches to her own drummer. I think that girl is still in there somewhere."

"Adam…" She turned to him. "What are we doing?"

"Having a conversation."

"You know what I mean. This banter. This…flirting. It's not real life. It's the whiskey and maybe a bit of adrenaline."

"So?"

"Don't you think we should call it a night?"

"Is that what you want?"

"No," she admitted. "And that worries me."

"Relax. Nothing's going to happen unless you want it to happen."

"That's the thing, though…" She turned back into him, lips parted invitingly, moonlight glinting in her eyes.

One minute, they were gazing knowingly at each other, and the next, she was astride him on the steps, kissing him fiercely as she tore at his shirt.

Chapter Fourteen

Somehow they made it into the house, stumbling up the steps, crashing recklessly into walls and then pausing in the kitchen for a kiss that ended with her on the counter, arms over her head as he tugged off her top. His shirt hung open. She slid it down his arms and threw it aside.

They were both breathing heavily by this time. Impatient and greedy, Adam nuzzled her neck and then her breasts as she leaned back on her hands. He unfastened her jeans and yanked them down her legs. She kicked out of them and then found his zipper.

It was wild. Exhilarating. Totally out of control. It had been too long, Nikki thought, and she slid off the counter. They dropped to the floor, laughing at her scraped elbow and his bumped knee, and then kissing, kissing, kissing. In a flash, she was astride him again, pushing aside her underwear to take him in.

"Damn, Nikki."

"I know."

They lay panting side by side on the cold tile.

"I really wasn't expecting the evening to end like this," she said.

"Gives new meaning to the term 'going out with a bang.'"

They lay on their backs gazing up at the ceiling, not quite touching as their breathing steadied. After a bit, Nikki reached for her jeans and shimmied into them. Adam did the same, and then they both lay back on the floor, not overly comfortable with one another, but not awkward, either. Nikki felt a little giddy. She wondered if it was the whiskey or the sex that made her feel so loose.

"What are you thinking?" Adam finally asked.

"The truth? That I'll never be able to sit at that counter without thinking of you with your pants down around your ankles."

"That's blunt. And you're welcome, by the way."

She laughed and couldn't seem to stop. "I think I'm drunk."

"On a few sips of whiskey?"

"How else do you explain the insanity?"

"Which part? The giggling or the kitchen sex?"

"All of it. I'm normally a very serious person."

He rolled onto his side and propped his elbow on the floor. "You have a serious job. But there's no harm in having a little fun now and then."

"That's not altogether true," Nikki said as she rubbed the back of her elbow. "We could have sprained something."

"We're not *that* old."

She sat up and stretched, and then reached for her top. "Maybe we should at least move to a more comfortable location. These tiles are hard and cold. Or, you know, we could just call it a night."

"You're kicking me out?" he asked lazily.

"No. I'm giving you an easy exit."

"Maybe I don't want an easy exit." He finished dressing and then pulled her to her feet. "Come on. We left the whiskey out on the steps."

"Whiskey is the last thing I need right now," Nikki said. "I have work tomorrow."

"Just a nightcap and then I'll be on my way."

They went back outside and sat down on the steps. The breeze drifting through the garden was warm and fragrant, perfumed now by the moonflowers that had opened to the night.

The whiskey went untouched. They sat in moonlit silence until Adam finally said, "I also have a confession to make."

Nikki turned with a scowl. "If you tell me you're married, I'll shoot you with your own gun."

He waggled his ringless finger. "Ex-fiancée, remember?"

She exaggerated her relieved sigh. "What's the confession?"

"I wasn't really surprised the other night at the Ruins when you found that watch."

Her head snapped around. "What? You knew the watch was there?"

"Let me rephrase that. The watch surprised me, but not the hiding place. I knew about that loose floorboard."

Her heart thudded as their gazes met in the dark.

"I came across it that summer while searching for clues. There was a notebook inside. A journal."

She closed her eyes briefly. "I always wondered. It's like how you can tell when someone has been in your house. I just knew somehow." She stared up at the moon. "You read it?"

"Yes."

"All of it?"

"I found a handwritten journal hidden beneath the floorboards of an abandoned mental hospital. What do you think?"

She glanced back at him. "You didn't say anything that summer. Why tell me now?"

"Because I don't like secrets."

She dropped her gaze to the garden, where shadows danced gently against the fence. "So you've known all along what I did."

"I know that you talked to Riley Cavanaugh on the night she disappeared. You may have been one of the last people to see her alive and yet you never went to the cops. Yeah, I know all that. But for what it's worth coming from me, you didn't do anything wrong."

He sought her gaze in the moonlight, but she avoided the contact, keeping her focus on the shadows instead. "I know I didn't do anything wrong, but I didn't do the right thing, either. She came to me that night. *Me*. Because I was the only one who could help her. At least that's what she thought. She and her friends had been dared to go out to the Ruins and she said she wanted to make sure the place was safe. She'd heard that I went out there a lot. She asked if I'd ever seen Preacher there. But that's not really why she came to me. She wasn't seeking reassurance. She was scared and she wanted me to give her an easy out. A way to save face with her friends. But instead, I told her she should take the dare. There was nothing to be afraid of at the Ruins. It was a beautiful place by moonlight."

"You couldn't have known what would happen." Adam put his hand on her knee, squeezing ever so lightly. The gesture was intimate and comforting.

Nikki drew a breath and nodded. "I know that. Rationally, I know her disappearance wasn't my fault, but I also know that if I'd told her not to go, she would probably still be alive. Married with a family, maybe. An interesting career. And Jenna Malloy wouldn't have spent the past fifteen years in and out of psychiatric facilities."

"You didn't make those girls go out to the Ruins, Nikki. It was like a rite of passage back then. They probably would have gone regardless of what you said."

"We'll never know. But it wasn't just my guilt that kept me silent. Tom Brannon's father was the sheriff. He considered me a person of interest. People were already whispering that the Belle Pointe Five had lured those poor girls to the Ruins for some dark purpose on the night of a blood moon. I was scared of what would happen if anyone found out that I'd talked to Riley before she disappeared, much less that I'd encouraged her to take that dare."

"So you wrote it all out in your journal. That was your confession."

"I took the coward's way out," she said. "Withholding information in a police investigation is illegal. If anyone had ever found out, my scholarships would have been rescinded. So I kept my mouth shut."

"What do you think happened to your journal? I assume that's why you went to the Ruins the other night."

"Whoever put Dr. Nance's watch under the floorboards must have taken it. I can only assume they've read it by now."

"Yes, and if they'd wanted to use it against you, they would have already done so."

"Unless they're keeping it for another reason."

"What reason would that be?"

Nikki shivered. "I don't know. I just have a bad feeling that journal is going to come back to haunt me."

Chapter Fifteen

Nikki arrived at work early the next morning and threw herself into the day's tasks, letting the autopsies and routine paperwork occupy her hands and her mind. She didn't talk to Adam all day. She assumed he was out replacing his phone and she hoped he had enough sense to stay away from the salvage yard. He was a grown man, though, and she reminded herself that she couldn't worry about his every move. She had her own concerns.

Still, his silence niggled. Despite that, the day flew by and she got so much accomplished that she considered taking off an hour or two early. But then Tom Brannon called. Seeing his name on her phone was never a good sign.

"Hey, Tom. What's up?"

"We've got another body, Nikki. How soon can you get here?"

"Where are you?"

"Ten miles east of town on Highway 30. I'll text you the address."

"It'll take me a good half hour and that's if I don't hit traffic. Have you ID'd the victim?"

"Yeah," he said grimly. "It's Eddie Bowman."

Nikki gasped. "The junkman, Eddie Bowman?"

"Can't say I'm surprised. That guy has been living on borrowed time for years."

Nikki clutched the phone. "What happened?"

"Looks like someone capped him in the chest a couple of times. We've got the place locked down. No one in or out until you get here."

Nikki signed out and checked her kit to make sure she had everything she needed. Then she headed out to the salvage yard. Traffic was light and she made good time. A sheriff's deputy let her in the first gate and Sheriff Brannon met her at the second. He filled her in as she pulled coveralls over her clothes and grabbed her kit. They both paused at the door to the office to put on gloves and plastic booties. Then he led her inside.

The body lay on the floor in the cramped office. Blood had soaked through his clothes and pooled on the linoleum. Nikki knelt and began her preliminary examination while Tom looked on. First, she checked to see if Bowman wore a watch. If damaged in a scuffle or fall, a stopped timepiece could give an accurate time of death. He wasn't, so she went on to the next step, measuring the wounds as she pointed out to Billy Navarro where and how to shoot the necessary photos.

"Looks like a 9mm," Nikki said. "Close range." She glanced around. "No sign of a struggle. He was shot in the chest, so he must have seen his killer. Probably knew him, too. Who called it in?"

"A guy came out here looking for a carburetor for a '68 Impala. Said he had an appointment. When he got here, the dogs were raising all kinds of hell, but they were penned up, so he didn't pay them much mind. Said he hollered for Bowman and then went into the office to look for him. That's when he saw the body."

"What time was this?"

"Right around two in the afternoon."

Nikki nodded. "Going by the body temp, I'd say he was shot sometime early this morning, but I can give you a better estimate once we get him back to the lab."

She glanced around, taking in the cramped, cluttered space and allowing herself to think about the unthinkable for one split second. Where was Adam? Had he come back out here to search the office? Would the police find his fingerprints all over the desk and possibly the body?

Crazy to even have such thoughts. She shook herself and went back to work, collecting samples and directing Navarro's photography.

Meanwhile, Tom Brannon had opened one of the desk drawers. "Take a look at this."

Nikki didn't know if he meant her, Billy Navarro or the crime scene personnel who were busy collecting trace evidence. She got up and went to have a look. There were several envelopes inside, all stuffed with cash.

"He didn't get this selling old carburetors," Tom said. "Doesn't look like robbery was a motive. A drug deal gone bad, most likely."

"Or possibly he was into the blackmail business," Nikki said.

Tom glanced up. "You know something I don't?"

"Yes, and you're not going to like it."

ADAM WAS ON his way back from Dallas when he got the call from Nikki on his new phone. He pulled off the freeway and called her back. She sounded upset.

"Where have you been? I've been trying to reach you for hours."

"I had some business to take care of in Dallas." He'd picked up his mail at the apartment, checked in with his lieutenant. He'd even called Dr. Cassidy to schedule a session. Time to start thinking about getting his life back in order. All those loose ends had kept him tethered to the past. "I'm on my way back to Belle Pointe now."

"What were you doing in Dallas? Never mind. That's none of my business and we've more pressing matters at the moment." She paused to draw a breath. "I've just come from the salvage yard. Eddie Bowman was found dead this afternoon."

Adam was glad he'd pulled over. "What happened?"

"He was shot twice in the chest at close range. I'm at the lab now. I'll be here for a few more hours."

"Are there any suspects?"

She hesitated. "I told Tom Brannon about your run-in yesterday with Bowman. I had to. I also told him everything else we've discovered. It's all conjecture at this point, but he needed to know."

"You did the right thing. Call me when you're leaving the lab. We'll meet and figure out where to go from here."

"Tom will want to talk to you."

"I'll go straight to the station as soon as I get to town." He paused. "Nikki? Be careful. Somebody may be tying up loose ends. We need to figure this thing out before the body count rises in Belle Point."

BY THE TIME Adam finished at the station with Sheriff Brannon, twilight had fallen. He called to check in with Nikki. She was still at the lab and would be for another hour or so. He drove back out to the lake and sat down at his grandmother's kitchen table to go through the bag of mail his super had collected from his overflowing mailbox.

He sorted through the usual flyers and bills until he came to a large, thick envelope marked Private and Confidential. The postmark was from more than a week ago. Probably arrived a day or two after he'd left for Belle Pointe. He used his pocketknife to slice the packing tape and then carefully removed a book from the wrapper. It was an old edition of *The Talented Mr. Ripley*. Adam had no idea what the significance of the title was, but he had no doubt the book had been sent by Dr. Nance.

He leafed through the pages and then carefully examined the binding. Sure enough, a tiny rolled note had been pushed up through an opening in the spine. He fished out the note, which contained two words: *Oak Lane*.

IT WAS DARK by the time Nikki left the lab. She was bone-deep tired and wanted nothing more than to go home, crawl between the sheets and sleep until sunrise. She thought about calling Adam to let him know she was on her way, but she decided to wait and call him from home. Traffic was still a little heavy in places and she needed to stay focused on the road.

A few miles from Belle Pointe, she began to suspect someone was following her. The headlights had stayed a consistent distance behind her ever since she'd left the lab. She hadn't paid much attention until the traffic thinned and suddenly there were only two vehicles on the road.

Nikki sped up, letting the needle climb to eighty-five before she backed off as she approached a sharp curve. She rounded the hairpin turn too quickly and nearly lost control of the wheel before she tapped the brakes and slowed. She came out of the turn and glanced behind her. The vehicle made the curve and gained on her. She could see now that it was a truck. She couldn't tell the make or model, but she had an image of an old panel truck covered in primer.

She used the voice control on her Bluetooth to call Adam. He answered on the first ring.

"Someone's following me," she said.

"Where are you?"

She gave him her approximate location as she split her attention between the road and the rearview.

"I'm on my way," he said. "Whatever you do, don't pull over. Keep driving. I'm coming to meet you."

The truck butted her bumper and Nikki gasped as she clutched the wheel.

"Nikki? What happened? Are you still there?"

"He just rammed my bumper. I have to go."

"Speed up. See if you can outrun him. Just hang in there…"

Nikki floored the accelerator and her SUV shot forward. As long as the road remained straight, she would be fine. She could outpace the older, heavier vehicle, but they were coming up on another turn. She couldn't make it at this speed. She had to slow down—

The truck struck her bumper again, this time hard enough that Nikki momentarily lost control. As they rounded the curve, the truck drew even with her and then swerved into her, forcing her off the road. She fought the wheel and almost had control before her tires spun out on loose gravel. Her SUV mowed down a road sign before bumping headlong down the embankment to crash into a tree.

WHEN NIKKI CAME to she was lying on her side out in the open. She thought at first that someone had pulled her from the wrecked vehicle and left her in the woods. But she wasn't alone. She could hear a strange, rhythmic sound in the background. She tried to lift a hand to her throbbing temple, but she couldn't move. A wave of terror washed over her. Had she been paralyzed in the accident? Then she realized that her hands and ankles were bound and a gag had been tied around her mouth. She wasn't on the side of the road at all but back home in her garden. She could smell the roses. Was she dreaming?

That rhythmic sound. What was it? A metallic strike followed by a soft thud. And in between, the sound of labored breathing.

Digging. Someone was digging in one of her flower beds. At this time of night?

She tried to maneuver to a sitting position, scooting her body around until she could pinpoint her location. Nothing looked familiar. She wasn't in her yard after all.

Where am I?

A scream rose to her throat, stifled by the gag.

She fell back on the ground, hyperventilating. She forced herself to stay calm. To take deep, slow breaths. Once the haze started to clear she was only too aware of her predicament. She'd been forced off the road and knocked out by the crash. She'd been taken. Just as Riley Cavanaugh had been taken all those years ago. Taken by some unknown assailant who was now digging her grave.

Panic enveloped her again and she had to remind herself to breathe slowly. Help would be coming for her soon. Adam knew her approximate location on the road. He would already be looking for her. He'd find her car and know that she was in trouble. He could trace her current location using the GPS on her phone, except...was her phone still in her vehicle?

Think, Nikki, think! You can do this.

She'd been on her own for as long as she could remember. She could find a way out. She had to.

She lay quietly for a moment as she worked at the cord around her wrist. It was wrapped tightly, but there was a slight give in the fabric. *Just keep working it. Don't make a sound.*

The point of the shovel struck the ground in front of her. Nikki looked up into the cold blue eyes staring down at her.

Then Lila Wilkes squatted and brushed the hair from Nikki's face. She tried to jerk away but the woman grasped her chin. "Hold still. You've got some dirt on your cheek." She licked a finger and rubbed at the smudge.

Nikki recoiled in revulsion and horror.

"You must be wondering what you're doing here," Lila said in a conversational voice. "Or have you figured it all out by now? I knew it would just be a matter of time. Once you found all those clues poor Charles left behind, you'd put it all together. You've always been a clever girl, haven't you? Do you want to know how *I* put it all together?"

Nikki shook her head and tried to roll out of the woman's reach.

"Sure you do. I found his diary. I found yours, too, as a matter of fact, but we'll get to that later. We're talking about Charles right now. He wrote it all down in his journal. Not in so many words, mind you. That was a bit of a puzzle, too, but when you know someone for as long and as well as I knew Charles Nance, you get how their mind works. Even when that mind starts to slip. The connection is still there. The onset of dementia just made things a bit fuzzy. Do you know what I mean?"

Nikki stared at her in horror as she worked at the bindings.

"You must have a lot of questions. I'll tell you everything before you go," Lila said. "You deserve that and I've always been a good storyteller. I'm a good actress, too. I have lots of talents that no one knows about. No one alive. You're in a unique position, Nikki. The others were either too lost in dementia or too ravaged by disease and old age to appreciate what I've gone through. But you're different. Still young and vibrant.

Still of sound mind. And you come from a dark past, too. We both carry that darkness inside of us. I used to think that if I'd ever had a daughter, I'd want her to be just like you."

Nikki shook her head violently, denying any sort of similarity or connection to the woman.

Lila lowered herself to the ground, settling in. "You already know the part about Charles bringing me here to care for my sick aunt, but I skipped part of the story. I took a bus from Baton Rouge to Belle Pointe and that's actually the most important part. I met a young woman on that bus. She was alone, like me. A shy, sad widow on her way to a small town in East Texas to care for her sick aunt. Her name, she said, was Lila Wilkes."

Sweat trickled down Nikki's face as she struggled with the bindings.

"I won't bore you with the details of my real identity. Suffice to say, I was on that bus fleeing from an uncomfortable situation. I needed a place where I could lie low for a while. Take a new name, get my hands on some cash. When I followed Lila off the bus, I never meant to stay in Belle Pointe. But then I realized that no one knew what she looked like. We were roughly the same age, the same build. Even Aunt Mary didn't suspect a thing. Not at first. I buried Lila beneath Mary's favorite rosebush. Twilight Mist. Isn't that the loveliest name for a rose? I used to cut the fresh buds and put them in my aunt's bedroom so she could watch them open. After a while, she began to look at me different, and I knew she suspected the truth. Not that it mattered, of course. She couldn't tell anyone about me. Couldn't speak, couldn't write. Could only lie quietly and follow me with her eyes. One day I noticed something strange about her. The horror in her eyes had turned to grudging admiration and, dare I say, affection. She needed me and I needed her. The arrangement suited us both. Honestly, I was quite upset when she passed. I'd become very fond of her."

A car sounded on the street. Lila straightened in alarm and then hunkered back down as the vehicle passed. "False alarm. No one will think to look for you in my backyard. Why would they? I'm the town's guardian angel."

The horror and helplessness of Nikki's predicament were starting to weigh on her. The woman was right. Who would think to look for her here? Who would ever suspect Lila Wilkes?

"I was surprised to find how much I liked Belle Pointe. Such a sleepy little town. Off the beaten path. A perfect place to hide from my past. I was no longer the girl who had stabbed her boyfriend in the eye with an ice pick. Here, I was an angel of mercy. Offering the sick and infirm a painless demise, followed by a beautiful send-off." She clasped her hands. "Only two people in this town ever suspected a thing. It took Charles Nance years to put it together, but your grandmother had me pegged from the moment she clapped eyes on me."

Nikki froze. Her eyes widened.

Lila laughed softly. "She really was quite something. Tough as nails, that woman. I liked her. She despised me, of course, but I respected that. She always suspected something was off, but I don't think she realized my true capabilities until her neighbor died.

"I'd been looking after poor Mrs. McHenry for months. Like my aunt, a stroke had debilitated her. I helped her make the transition by putting a pillow over her face. Your grandmother confronted me. This was after you'd gone off to college, so she was alone in the house. It would have been easy enough to shut her up for good, but that could have aroused suspicion coming so soon after her neighbor's death. So I took that watch from Charles's study and planted it beneath the floorboard at the Ruins."

Nikki physically started at the revelation.

Lila nodded at her reaction. "Yes, I knew all about your little hiding place. I know everything that goes on in this town. I told your grandmother if she made trouble for me, I'd see to it that you got blamed for stealing that watch. I'd show the sheriff your journal, too. You know, the part where you'd been with Riley Cavanaugh the night she disappeared? Even if you didn't do jail time, you'd lose all your scholarship and grant money. You'd have to drop out of school and would likely end up like your worthless mother. So your grandmother kept silent. She went to her grave protecting you, Nikki. You should be very proud of her."

Tears stung Nikki's eyes. She tried to summon her grandmother's spirit. She had been tough as nails. What would she do in Nikki's position?

Stop struggling so hard against those bindings, girl. You're only tightening the knot. Just slow down and take your time. Use your head for a change.

Nikki calmed herself yet again and worked methodically at the knot. Maybe it was her imagination, but the cord seemed looser around her wrists.

"So that's my story." Lila smiled down at her in the moonlight. "I've answered all your questions and given you the gift of your grandmother's devotion. See? I really am an angel. And now to be merciful…"

Nikki shook her head, silently pleading.

"Don't worry," Lila soothed. "It'll be painless. I could just knock you in the head, throw you in the grave and bury you alive the way I did poor Lila, but I have more refined sensibilities now." She produced a gun from the pocket of her jeans. "See? It has a silencer and everything. One shot between the eyes and you won't feel a thing. Eddie Bowman procured it for me and I used it just this morning to shoot him in the chest. He was useful to a certain point, but stupid and greedy. Willing to do almost anything for the right amount of money, but then he'd turn around and blackmail you for the rest of your life if you let him. Ask Dr. Wingate about that. I knew when I hired him to help dispose of Dr. Nance's body that I would have to get rid of him, too. I was careful about leaving fingerprints in his office, but I can't say the same about Dr. Wingate. I expect she's in for a rough few weeks, especially if I decide to plant this gun in her house. But we have to deal with you first, don't we?" She stuffed the gun back in her capris and grabbed Nikki's bound feet. "Let's get you in the hole. Be less messy that way."

She was strong for her age. Strong for any age. She picked up Nikki's bound feet and dragged her with relative ease to the grave. Nikki went limp until Lila stood near the edge, and then she bucked her body and kicked. The attack seemed to catch Lila by surprise. She was used to a more fragile victim. She teetered on the edge and then fell backward into the grave.

Nikki scrambled away, slipping her hands free of the cord, ripping off the gag, and then she set to work on her ankles. Before she could free herself completely, Lila hoisted herself out of the grave. Grasping the gun in both hands, she staggered to her feet, looking desperate and demented in the moonlight. Nikki ducked and rolled, trying to make herself a harder target to hit.

Adam seemed to appear out of nowhere. In actuality, he'd slipped through the back gate without either of them noticing. He picked up the shovel and whacked Lila Wilkes on the back of the head. She hit the ground with a soft thud.

He was beside Nikki in a flash, untying her ankles and then taking her face in his hands. "You okay?"

"I am now," she said. "How did you know where to find me?"

"Dr. Nance left us the address."

"What?"

"1447 Oak Lane. He led me straight to his killer."

Chapter Sixteen

Nikki spent the rest of the night and most of the next day in the hospital undergoing a round of tests to make certain she'd suffered no internal injuries from the accident. Adam stayed with her the whole time and they both gave their statements to Tom Brannon at her bedside.

That afternoon, Adam drove her home and fussed over her until she finally said, "Enough. I feel fine. Let's go sit outside and get some fresh air."

They sat on the back steps taking in the lush scent of the roses as they watched a glorious sunset. After a while, they talked about everything that had happened.

"Turns out, Lila Wilkes, aka Sally Johnston, spent some time in a mental health facility when she was a teenager," Adam said. "That's probably why she was so fascinated with the Ruins."

"As much time as I spent out there as a kid, I never once saw her," Nikki said.

"She was careful. She went in and out of Dr. Nance's house without Dessie ever seeing her. She was probably in a lot of other houses, too. She kept tabs on everyone. Tom Brannon showed me photos of the stacks and stacks of journals they found in her house, detailing everything she's done. She's still quite proud of herself and seems to be enjoying all the attention."

Nikki shivered. "It's chilling to think how she watched us for years. How she literally got away with murder right under our noses. And everyone called her an angel. No one suspected a thing. Why do you think she did it?"

"Other than being criminally insane? She craved the attention, especially as she got older. She won praises for caring for the elderly and more praises still for planning their funerals. I guess you could say she found her niche."

Nikki gave him a look. "The woman is a cold-blooded killer. She stabbed her boyfriend in the eye with an ice pick."

"I'm not making light of what she did," Adam said. "Far from it."

They were sitting close, touching comfortably. Adam put his hand on her knee and she laid her head on his shoulder. "This town has been through so much in the past fifteen years. We never got over Riley's disappearance and now this. Our most beloved citizen murdered by our second most beloved citizen. A woman who was never who we thought she was. My grandmother knew all along and she never said a word."

"She didn't know. She suspected. She had no proof. She kept silent to protect you."

"That's something I'm still trying to digest," Nikki said. "I always thought I was just an annoyance to her. A burden. Turns out—"

"She loved you."

Nikki blinked back hot tears. "I wish I'd known."

"You know now. You can't go back in time, Nikki. You can only move forward."

She sighed. "What happens now?"

"Things will get back to normal eventually. Dr. Wingate will probably be investigated. As for Dessie and Clete…" He shrugged. "Maybe they'll make a go of it. Dr. Nance's will seems to be legit. Dessie gets the house and enough cash to live comfortably. Your school loans will be taken care of. The rest goes to research. He was a good man, Dr. Nance."

"A very good man." She turned to search Adam's features. "But I meant, what happens to us? There's nothing keeping you here now that you've solved Dr. Nance's mystery."

Adam squeezed her knee. "I wouldn't say *nothing*."

"You know what I mean. I assume you'll be heading back to Dallas in a few days. You'll get your old job back and your life will return to normal, too."

"You make it sound like normal has to be the end of things," he said. "Dallas is little more than a two-hour drive from Belle Pointe. I sometimes sit longer than that in traffic. We can see each other whenever we want. *If* we want. Maybe we can even try dating. You know, dinner, movies, baseball games." He shrugged. "I say, we see how it plays out."

Nikki thought about his suggestion. She'd rarely ever made time for a social life. She'd devoted herself to her studies and then to her career. She had a vision of herself in the lab, the hours flying by until it was time to leave the lab and go meet Adam for dinner. Or a movie. Or a baseball game. Or just a leisurely evening here in her garden. For now, it sounded like the best of both worlds. It sounded a little bit like heaven.

She nodded, her head still nuzzled against his shoulder. "Yeah," she said. "Let's see how it plays out."

* * * * *

*Look for the thrilling conclusion of Echo Lake
by Amanda Stevens.*
Someone Is Watching *available for preorder
wherever Harlequin Intrigue books
are sold.*

*Finding a baby on his doorstep is the last thing
Texas Ranger Eli Slater expects in the middle of the
night. Until he discovers that his ex, Ashlyn Darrow,
is the little girl's mother and the child was just
kidnapped from her. Now they have to figure out who's
behind this heinous crime while trying very hard to
keep their hands off each other…*

Keep reading for a sneak peek at
Settling an Old Score,
part of Longview Ridge Ranch,
from USA TODAY *bestselling author Delores Fossen.*

"Two cops broke into your house?" He didn't bother to take out the
skepticism. "Did they have a warrant? Did they ID themselves?"

Ashlyn shook her head. "They were wearing uniforms, badges
and all the gear that cops have. They used a stun gun on me." She
rubbed her fingers along the side of her arm, and the trembling got
worse. "They took Cora, but I heard them say they were working
for you."

Eli's groan was even louder than the one she made. "And you
believed them." The look he gave her was as flat as his tone. He
didn't spell out to her that she'd been gullible, but he was certain
Ashlyn had already picked up on that.

She squeezed her eyes shut a moment. "I panicked. Wasn't
thinking straight. As soon as I could move, I jumped in my car and
drove straight here."

The drive wouldn't have taken that long since Ashlyn's house
was only about ten miles away. She lived on a small ranch on
the other side of Longview Ridge that she'd inherited from her
grandparents, and she made a living training and boarding horses.

"Did the kidnappers make a ransom demand?" he pressed. "Or did they take anything else from your place?"

"No. They only took Cora. Who brought her here?" Ashlyn asked, her head whipping up. "Was it those cops?"

"Fake cops," Eli automatically corrected. "I didn't see who left her on my porch, but they weren't exactly quiet about it. She was probably out here no more than a minute or two before I went to the door and found her."

He paused, worked through the pieces that she'd just given him and it didn't take him long to come to a conclusion. A bad one. These fake cops hadn't hurt the child, hadn't asked for money or taken anything, but they had let Ashlyn believe they worked for him. There had to be a good reason for that. Well, "good" in their minds, anyway.

"This was some kind of sick game?" she asked.

It was looking that way. A game designed to send her after him.

"They wanted me to kill you?" Ashlyn added a moment later.

Before Eli answered that, he wanted to talk to his brother and get backup so he could take Ashlyn and the baby into Longview Ridge. First to the hospital to confirm they were okay and then to the sheriff's office so he could get an official statement from Ashlyn.

"You really had no part in this?" she pressed.

Eli huffed, not bothering to answer that. He took out his phone to make that call to Kellan, but he stopped when he saw the blur of motion on the other side of Ashlyn's car. He lifted his hand to silence her when Ashlyn started to speak, and he kept looking.

Waiting.

Then, he finally saw it. Or rather he saw them. Two men wearing uniforms, and they had guns aimed right at the house.

Don't miss
Settling an Old Score *by Delores Fossen,*
available August 2020 wherever
Harlequin Intrigue books and ebooks are sold.

Harlequin.com

Love Harlequin romance?

DISCOVER.
Be the first to find out about promotions, news and exclusive content!

Facebook.com/HarlequinBooks

Twitter.com/HarlequinBooks

Instagram.com/HarlequinBooks

Pinterest.com/HarlequinBooks

ReaderService.com

EXPLORE.
Sign up for the Harlequin e-newsletter and download a free book from any series at
TryHarlequin.com

CONNECT.
Join our Harlequin community to share your thoughts and connect with other romance readers!
Facebook.com/groups/HarlequinConnection

HSOCIAL2020